SONG OF FREEDOM, SONG OF DREAMS

Also by Shari Green

Root Beer Candy and Other Miracles

Macy McMillan and the Rainbow Goddess

Missing Mike

Game Face

SONG OF FREEDOM, SONG OF DREAMS

A NOVEL IN VERSE

Shari Green

Andrews McMeel
PUBLISHING®

Andrews McMeel Publishing
a division of Andrews McMeel Universal
1130 Walnut Street, Kansas City, Missouri 64106

www.andrewsmcmeel.com

24 25 26 27 28 TEN 10 9 8 7 6 5 4 3 2 1

Paperback ISBN: 978-1-5248-8112-2
Hardcover ISBN: 978-1-5248-8113-9

Library of Congress Control Number: 2023940278

Editor: Patty Rice
Art Director/Designer: Tiffany Meairs
Production Editor: David Shaw
Production Manager: Shona Burns

ATTENTION: SCHOOLS AND BUSINESSES

Andrews McMeel books are available at quantity discounts with bulk purchase for educational, business, or sales promotional use. For information, please e-mail the Andrews McMeel Publishing Special Sales Department:
sales@amuniversal.com.

For Heather

Tune our hearts to brave music

—from a prayer of Saint Augustine

Leipzig, German Democratic Republic
August 1989

Helena:

I've not been raised to speak
of dreams—nor to dream
at all. There is no need.

Already at sixteen, the path
for my future is clear.
The same is true for Katrin
—for all of us.
There will always be jobs
here, unlike the West.
Always a place to live and a way
to contribute. What more
could we want?

But I do want. Secretly
      quietly
              in the deepest
corner of my heart

      I want.

I'm not the only dreamer
in the family. Some nights when I'm hidden
away, studying in my room
I hear my parents
talking low, cautious of thin walls
betraying their secrets to neighbors

      —neighbors who may latch
      onto scraps and scurry
      to the government, trade them
      for small luxuries
          or to save their own skin.

Mama's and Papa's dreams are different
from mine. Papa whispers words
like *electoral reform*
but Mama, if pressed
will only admit to a longing
for simpler things—more choices
in the shops, the ability
to purchase bananas
      oranges, even
like she remembers having
when she was young

but in the morning
dreams vanish.

My parents greet me wearing masks
of contentment as we share
an orange-free breakfast.

Katrin convinces me to postpone
practice. Despite fingers itching
to play, I leave my piano,
and Katrin and I spend the afternoon
riding streetcars, our destination
guided by a game we invented
when we were first old enough
to venture out on our own—*off*
when we hear mention
of Herr Honecker, *on*
when we see an image of his face.
You can go a long way like that.

We're not fool enough to let other
passengers catch on to the fact
we've made a game
     of the leader
of the German Democratic Republic

     but our secret daring
     delights us.

We call it quits when we find
ourselves near Karl-Marx-Platz.
Katrin seems weary
of the game by then. Perhaps
we've outgrown it, although
when we began today, we were both
as keen as ever. No, it was the mood
in the streetcars that was the thief
of joy

        unease
simmering
like a distant storm.

We disembark, breathe the coal-
dusted air as if it marks a great improvement
from that of the tram. After wandering
toward the fountain in the square
we claim an empty bench and settle
beside one another.

I sift through city noise, searching
for music rising
from the Gewandhaus beyond the statues
of the fountain. Days when the symphony
rehearses are my favorite. Today
the concert hall is quiet.

We're going camping
this weekend, Katrin says
out of the blue. *Lake Balaton.*

Lake Balaton!
I've hardly ever been out
of our Germany, but one summer
my parents took me to Hungary
for three glorious days
beside that sparkling expanse
of water.

You're so lucky, I say.

I'm lost for a moment in memories
of our family trip, so far removed
from the grime and growing
tension in the city, until Katrin turns
and faces me on the bench
clasps my hand
        voice earnest.

I'll miss you, she says.

A quick laugh bursts
from my throat.

Sure you will, I tease.
When you're not too busy
swimming and sunbathing.

Her expression grows
wistful. *I wish*
you were going with me.

We don't often go to church
as a family, but from time
to time, I visit the Thomaskirche
where Wagner studied, Mozart
once played, and Bach himself
was choirmaster. I go less
for the worship and more
to be transported
by some spectral shadow
of the masters
wafting from the pipes.

Sunday morning, I slip
into the sanctuary early
before the service begins, settle
on a smooth wooden seat
near the back. Even in the silence
I hear music.

It winds around pillars
and pews, wends its way
beneath my skin and burrows
in my bones. It is exactly
the nourishment I need.

Nikolaikirche: 20 August
(*St. Nicholas Church, Leipzig*)

It has been said that to clasp the hands
in prayer is the beginning
of an uprising.

Even now, as the faithful
the hopeful
the discontent
pass through my doors
gathering
to pray, the breeze
brushing past my tower
whispers of an undeniable
beginning.

Helena, **Mama says, drawing my attention**
before nodding at the stack
of dripping dishes.
You've spent more time peering
at the clock than you have
drying dishes.

Sorry. I snatch a plate
from the rack but can't pull
my mind from wondering
if it's too late to drop in
on Katrin.

Mama reads my thoughts.
I don't think they're back yet,
she says. *Frau Vogel*
wasn't at the butcher's
when I stopped by
on the way home.
They were shorthanded, too—
the line-up stretched
            all down the block.

I frown. *Katrin said it was only*
for the weekend. Didn't she?

Car trouble maybe, says Mama.
She reaches for the tail
of my dish towel, dries her hands.
I'm sure she'll stop by
once they're home.

8

Car trouble—of course.
Those Trabis are always breaking
down. Imagine waiting ten years
for a chance to buy something
that's broken more often
than it's working. No wonder
Papa can't be bothered.

If we had a telephone, I say
with a pointed look at Mama,
she could call *me*
when they return.

*Who do you know that's got
a phone?* Mama says
calling my bluff. *Certainly not
the Vogels.*

Papa returns from his evening
walk, beckons me
to come close. When he speaks
his voice is so low, I need to lean in.

I heard news, he says.

Western news, he means. Otherwise
there'd be no need to keep quiet.
Papa often comes home with tidbits
of news from the West, his walks
obviously less about exercise and more
about gathering "unauthorized"
information.

There was an event in Hungary
on the weekend, he says now. *A picnic*
near the border of Austria.
They opened the border
for a few hours—

My eyes widen.

It was planned, he says,
so delegations from both countries
could cross over. A gesture
of friendship.

He hesitates until I prod.

And?

And apparently, many from our country
took advantage
of the opportunity. Hundreds
fled into Austria
before they sealed the border.

It occurred to me—

No, I say. *No.*

I step back, ending
the conversation. What a foolish thought.
Katrin would've told me
if they'd planned to defect. Besides

they'd never want to leave.
Why would they?

That night I lie awake
in the dark, hoping
for sleep but instead pestered
by the memory of Katrin's declaration
the last time we were together:

    I'll miss you.

When I wake, my head
aches. I fight to push aside
the thoughts worming their way
into my consciousness
because they're ridiculous and
absolutely wrong.

Mama has already left
for the "tin can"—
            the aluminum-clad store
where she spends her days selling
GDR-approved clothing, helping customers
be their fashion-free best.

Papa sits reading in the sunlight
streaming through the open living room
window. He's left out breakfast
for me, but I ignore it, tell him I'm off
and head out before he can delay me.

I rush to the streetcar
silently urge
            hurryhurry

leap off at the stop nearest
Katrin's apartment block
and dash up the stairs.

I pound on the door, heart thumping
as loudly as my fists.

Surely Frau Vogel is about to swing
open the door, shoot a glare
my way because of the racket
I'm making, then usher me inside.
I'll find Katrin
in the room she shares
with her little sister.

Our stupid car, she'll say, or
I've been sick since
we got back—
nothing serious, but I couldn't
come over. I'll laugh
at my foolishness.

But a minute passes
            then two

and no one answers the door.

It could mean nothing

        or

        it could mean
everything.

I begin with scales
one after another, up
and down the keys, again
and again.

Then, a few hymns
some Mendelssohn
     Liszt
          Bach
half an hour
     an hour
          two

until all the unrest
within me works its way
to my fingers, flows
onto the keys

          and slips away.

Some evenings while I play
the piano, Papa gets out
his violin, stands behind me, raises
his bow, and it's all I can do
to keep playing instead of closing
my eyes, lifting my hands
from the keys to dance
in the air, conducting
the concerto or caprice.
I love the piano
        need the piano
but even more, I simply love

music. Nights when we play together
Mama closes her book or sets aside
her embroidery and listens.

See Mama, I said one night
after the music ended.
You love music as much
as Papa and I do.

It's the togetherness
I love, she said.
I would sit and listen
to you two conjugate Latin verbs
if you were doing it
together.

Music is good for the soul, Mama.
Like art and theater
and books. We need *music.*

Mama's face darkened.
We may like *music,* she said.
But we would not die
without it.

She's wrong. So wrong.

A part of me would most definitely
die without music.

It's been a week since the Vogels
headed to Lake Balaton.

If the car had broken down
                    surely by now
they'd have found another way home.

If there'd been an accident
            a tragedy of some sort
            surely by now
we'd have received word.

I've taken to checking their apartment
each day, then stopping
by the butcher shop to ask
after Frau Vogel. Each day her coworkers tell me
she's not returned to her job

and each day
my gut tells me
she never will.

We were thirteen the summer
a rare visit from Katrin's Frankfurt relatives
—aunt, uncle, their two boys
      a little older
than we were—stole Katrin away
from me for a whole week. They'd finally left
to return to their home in the *other* Germany
      the western half
                of our divided
      country
and Katrin and I were together
again. She grabbed my hand
      pulled me
into her room.

We dropped cross-legged
to her bedroom floor. She tugged
the quilt from her bed and we huddled
beneath it, cassette recorder between us
          volume low
          eyes and smiles wide
as we absorbed the contraband
music—a collection of her cousins'
favorite songs by The Beatles

rewinding again and again
until we'd memorized the words
and could sing along *pianissimo*
in our patchwork hideaway:

Yellow Submarine

   All You Need Is Love

Let It Be.

Often, for months afterward,
one of us would quote lyrics
at random, savoring
our secret. At times I hoped my classmates
would overhear, that they might think me daring
      and wild
rather than strange.

    No doubt, many of them
had their own source
of music from beyond
the GDR, their own secrets, never
to be freely shared

      but I knew better
than to trust my fate
to my fellow students.

     Which ones
would rat me out?
     Which ones
would grow up to become wretched
informants?

I climb the stairs, discover
a patch of light halfway
down the dim hall
      an open door
—they're home!

        I rush
toward the Vogels' apartment
my pace suddenly *allegro*
      lively and bright
until a man's voice
      so unlike Herr Vogel's scratchy
      smoker's voice
          stops me. I creep

forward, planning to peek
around the doorway, but then
a second unfamiliar voice
      a thump
and a sound
like a drawer's contents
being emptied onto the floor.

A chill sweeps through
me, stealing breath and thickening
my blood. I need to turn
around, go back
the way I came, but
my legs are unwilling.

Wood bangs against
wood.   A clash
      of notes.
         A cry
leaps to my lips.
      Not Katrin's piano!

My hand flies to my mouth, holding
in my protest as my heart pounds
a thundering crescendo.

I turn, careen

toward the stairs

down two flights

hit the lower landing at a run
and crash open the door.

I don't look
                back.

I've always known
to be careful, to never assume
I'm *not* being

watched
      listened to
            reported on

but serious sit-downs with Mama
never prepared me for strangers
pawing through Katrin's things
like dogs digging
for bones they've no right
to devour.

If Katrin and her family
are really and truly gone
what do the Stasi care?

Hundreds—maybe thousands
have left the country illegally.
Why would they bother
with a factory man, a butcher shop
clerk, and two kids who know

to keep their mouths shut
about anything the Party
would find less than loyal.
Katrin's parents don't even attend
the Monday peace prayers
      like Papa does.
Katrin has never held to dreams
as I have, and her only clandestine
activity was once sneaking out
to a dance party I was too timid
to attend. Otherwise
      as far as I know
her family has no secrets.

If they're gone
what damage control
could possibly be on the minds
of the Stasi?

Unless they hope to discover
connections

      other seemingly content families
who might harbor dreams of stealing
across borders
      other fathers and mothers
and children who'd secretly
      (or not so secretly)
love to see a change
in our government, families who might
march in protest, families who might
cause trouble and make the Party
                look bad.

Families like mine.

The last week of August brings the return
of weekly piano lessons. Katrin and I
always went together
to Herr Weber's home—me, reading
or studying on the small sofa
in the foyer while she had her lesson
then switching places
when it was my turn.

Today I arrive alone, Katrin's absence
from her long-standing time slot
striking discord
in an already melancholy day.

The studio door is open
      the foyer
              empty.

I hesitate, unprepared
for how foreign it feels
to be here without her.

As I take my place
on the piano bench

absently run scales
to warm up

I'm oddly disconnected.

Here.
      But not.

My world has slipped
sideways, and if I had any sense
I'd latch onto the piano
right this moment, and hold on
for dear life.

September 1989

September first was always
going to bring change

paths
                    diverging

—for me, extended high school
in preparation for writing the Abitur

for Katrin, vocational training
            (she'd settle for anything
that would keep her from her mother's
chosen path working for a butcher
            the stench of blood lingering
on her clothes)

            but Katrin's disappearance
is more change
than I'd bargained for, shifting everything
into unfamiliar territory.

I recognize only a few students
from earlier years, and none
were particularly friendly with me then.
Ingrid, at least, offers a smile
of recognition, but she's quick
to strike up conversation
with the boy beside her
rather than reconnect
with me.

A sigh escapes my lips.

Settling into a new class
is infinitely more difficult
knowing I've no one
to swap stories with later.

25

Since I was little, I've wanted
to be the conductor
  of a symphony. I work
hard in school
  volunteer
with the children's orchestra
do what I can
  to keep up appearances
  at meetings
   of the Free German Youth
so the powers that control
my future will have no reason
to deny me.

Mama tries to steer me
toward nursing or teaching, sensible
careers fitting for a bright, young
woman in the German Democratic
Republic. *After all,* she tells me,
how many conductors
does Leipzig need?

I say let others serve
as nurses and teachers. Music
is what I have to give.
And no matter
what Mama thinks, Leipzig needs
music.
  Everyone deserves
to experience music in a way
that awakens their soul
that astounds with beauty
that strengthens them for
whatever battles lie within
   and without.

I don't need to make people dance
  others will ensure
  there is always music enough
  for that.
I want them instead
to fly

spirits lifting to rafters
carried on song, pressing
through to blue skies and freedom.

It's a rebellious thought
to stir people
to dreams. Imagining
the possibility lets loose
butterflies within me.

One morning
      months ago
I woke early, while the night
still clung to the sky,
and lay in my bed, listening
to the silence.

A note broke through
then another
and another
      blackbirds
beginning their song
ahead of the dawn.

I threw back the covers
crossed to my window
bare feet quiet on the cold floor.

      The heat to the building
      was out again.

I looked outside and imagined
the songbirds' score
written on star-speckled sky
as the music played on
      and on.

I wanted to wake Mama
and Papa, share this wonder
with them—like all beautiful things
the miracle of birdsong
should be shared. Yet I couldn't
bring myself to step away
from the window or to break
the spell by calling out, so I listened
alone.

It was magic.

I told Katrin later
about the pre-dawn concert
and she laughed lovingly.

Oh, Conductor, she said.
You were in your glory
weren't you?

Details emerge, whispered
fragments cobbled together, shaping
a story supported by the news
Papa heard:

a Pan-European Picnic

a fence cutting
the field in half

      Hungary on one side
Austria on the other

a gate opened
for a few
to pass through.

A stampede
of hundreds.

How does a person just up
and vanish from their best
friend's life? And where
does the best friend go
from there?

Everything's messed up
tangled together
and this piece

>   I snatch the music book
>   open in front of me
>   slap it down
>   on the top of the piano

is *not* helping.

This is the kind of problem
I'd work out with Katrin.
>   The irony stings.

I opt for a Mozart concerto
hoping it will unfurl my snarl
of emotions. I play the first
page   once
>   twice
>   three times.

The emotional knot
loosens, one thread emerging
as dominant:

>   anger.

It shapes itself into a burning
coal, fueled not by Katrin's
disappearance, but by

Herr Honecker
the Party
and the whole socialist
training that has made escape
artists of our citizens.

I'm midway through
the same page of the concerto
when a vigorous banging
      jolts me.

Frau Richter next door, pounding
on our adjoining wall
      an ungracious note
to tell me it's past nine
and would I please shut up.

      I leave the piece
unfinished

      turn out
the lamp.

My dreams began
with a gunshot.

I was only ten
when I overheard Papa weeping
as he shared news
with Mama:

> violence
> near the border.

He was a child,
Papa said, choking
on his words. *The same
age as Helena.*

Compelled, I inclined my ear
listened to Papa recount
the horror
in hushed tones

> a guard
> a bullet
> and a boy from Berlin

who would never return
home. Maybe my thoughts
should've been on the immense
sadness of it all, but
I could only wonder:

What was out there beyond
the wall, beyond the German
Democratic Republic
that a boy would believe
was worth the risk

of barbed wire
spotlights
guard dogs
guns

and death?

Sunday evening, several
of Papa's friends crowd
into our living room, including
Christoph
      my favorite.

Christoph feels more like family
than friend, his lined face
and frequent robust laugh
familiar
      and comforting.

Now, he slips me a small bar
of chocolate, hands Mama
a package of coffee. He winks
as Mama gapes.

My sister, he says. *She sends the best
care packages.*

Mama sets to brewing a pot, grinning
but probably wishing
she too had a sister
to send treats from the west
side of the wall.

As chatter settles into earnest
discussions, I disappear into my room
leaving the door ajar.
The talk touches on ethics
      theology
            politics
and finally lands
on the practical matter
of peaceful protest.
I lean into their words.

Everyone's gathering
in the square outside
the Nikolaikirche, Christoph says.
When the prayer service ends

we march.

Mama's voice
        stretched thin: *Is it safe*
to march? Surely
they won't allow it.

But Papa reminds her
there were small demonstrations
following Monday peace prayers
before the meetings stopped
for their summer recess.

Besides, he says, *the International Trade Fair*
is tomorrow. The city will be packed
with visitors, including foreign media.
Lots of foreign media. The timing
is perfect.

Papa seems unperturbed
by the fact it's only safe
to protest
when our government knows
the world is watching.
But for me this truth
adds fuel to the fire.

Papa dons his jacket
a short while after arriving
home from work. While Christoph
will be among those who wait
in the square, Papa plans to arrive in time
for the Monday prayers.
He attended often in the spring
but if he marched
after the meetings then, he kept it
from me. Perhaps now that I'm sixteen
       as old
       as his students
he's realized he need not hide
from me the extent
of his discontent
with our government.

Papa is almost out the door
when the ember
in my gut
       flares.

I want to go too.

It's Mama who responds.

Absolutely not, she says.
*The meetings are not
for young people.*

Church is for everyone, I say
feigning ignorance—the meeting
is not about church. Not for Papa
at least. Not for many of those
who come, according
to what I've overheard
from Papa.

They gather to unite
with like-minded souls

people who believe loving
their god means fighting
for justice and peace

people who understand loving
their country means working
to repair its brokenness.

But Mama's not convinced
marching could be the path
to change.

*Sunday morning church
is for everyone,* says Mama. *Now
you stay home.*

*It's prayer meetings and protests,
Mama. It's not
as if I'm putting my complaints
on paper to fall
into the wrong hands.*

Mama blanches.

I've gone too far.

I said

     no.

From the way Papa and his friends talk
when they gather in our home
they clearly believe fire
in one's spirit should fuel
transformation, shaping
a landscape of brokenness and injustice
into a source of light

but Mama has taught me
to stamp out sparks
before they take hold. She knows
flames can run wild
and destroy
even the one who simply wanted
to keep warm.

Nikolaikirche: 4 September

The Stasi have blocked streets
as if to minimize and contain
those who will march.
Nevertheless, my pews fill.

While those inside
sing, pray, bolster strength
others gather in my courtyard
waiting for my doors to open,
the parishioners to join
their ranks. Some are desperate
to leave the GDR
others determined to stay
two sides of the same coin
sharing the same core
yearning
for a better life.

The Stasi wait too
but the presence
of international media
will keep them in check.

Tonight, all shall be well.

I step into the foyer barely
on time for my lesson,
find the studio door
                    closed.

As I perch on the threadbare sofa
the final stanzas of a sonata
drift from within, followed
by Herr Weber's muffled voice.

After a minute the studio door
              cracks open
and my heart
leaps, expecting
              for a split second
Katrin
to step out like she did
week after week
              year after year
grinning at me and joking
about warming up the keys
for me, or giving
a telling look to warn
if Herr Weber
was in a rare foul mood.

But of course
it's not Katrin.

Instead, a boy emerges
              —almost a man, really
wavy haired and long
legged.

My heart
which had leapt
at the thought of Katrin
trips.

He closes the studio door
behind him, catches
my eye and grins.

You're his next pupil? he asks.

He's definitely older
than I am. But not too much
older. His jawline betrays
only a hint
of having to shave.

You're a piano student? he says
and I realize
I should respond.

Herr Weber has been my teacher
a long time. You're new.

Since when
has Herr Weber accepted
new students?

New to Herr Weber
but not to piano. He grins again
dances long fingers
in the air. His reach on the keys
must be half again greater
than mine.

I'm Lucas, he says.

Helena.

Well. See you next week.

Excuse me?

Next Tuesday. Same time
same place?

He waggles his eyebrows
befuddling me.

    I'm saved
when Herr Weber opens the door
nods in my direction, ready
for our lesson.

Sheet music spread
before me, I position
my hands. They play
without any thought
from me.

When the piece ends
Herr Weber is silent.

Finally, he speaks.
            Gently.
Again.

I play again, this time
remaining focused. The notes
are correct, timing disciplined

bar after bar
line after line

but I know without doubt
it isn't music—only notes.
Herr Weber stops me mid-
way through the piece.

*Why did you not
practice?* he asks.

*I did. I'm sorry. I'll
try again.*

I lift my hands, but he stops me.

*That's enough
for today,* he says.

But the lesson's only just started!

He smiles patiently
says nothing.

I did practice—really. But . . .

*Helena, there is no point
in playing if you don't bring
your heart to the piano.
Where has your heart been?
Where is it now?*

Herr Weber waits a beat.

Katrin?

You gave away her spot.

I mean it only as an observation
a simple fact of the matter
but I hear the accusatory tone
in my voice.

I twist around to face
Herr Weber—this man who's taught
both Katrin and me
since we were eight
years old. A measure of sorrow
is written in the lines of his face.

When I speak again
my words are barely more
than a whisper.

You don't think she's coming back.

Our government labels
all who choose to leave
      traitors
and all who associate with them
      suspicious.

It's no surprise, then, that the first days
of school, no one speaks
of Katrin. Many in this school
never knew her, of course
but news of the Vogels' vanishing
has gotten around. Still,
the students are wise enough
      or cautious enough
to guard their tongue. But
in my seat near the front
of the room, I sense curious stares boring
into the back of my head.

Finally, the fourth full day
when we're outside
on break, three girls
hover around me—including Ingrid
and Martina from my old school, girls
who never had the time of day
for the likes of me, suddenly
clamoring to hear
what I might have to say.

I have nothing to say.

And yet

my silence may be interpreted
to mean exactly
the truth:

my best friend
did not confide her plans
in me.

In addition to Ingrid and Martina
there are two boys here
from my old school. I've known these four
since we were young

      together in school
         five and a half days per week
      together on the grounds while wind
         whipped the State flag above us
      together in Young Pioneers
         and the Free German Youth
          —the FDJ.

But togetherness
has never suited me.

It's no surprise my preference
for solitude has often been
interpreted as unfriendliness.
      (Mind you, trust
      is required in friendship
      so perhaps I've been trained
         to be unfriendly.)
It didn't help that the older
we got, the less I had
in common with my classmates—
other girls consumed with chattering
about boys in high staccato tones
while the only topic I was passionate
enough to actually speak about
in a group
      the power and beauty
      of classical music
they found odd, found *me* odd
      and eventually

there was only Katrin.
She liked classical music well enough
but she had the social grace
to understand how to read
others' interest. I expect they never understood
why Katrin stuck with me.
But Katrin and I were like sisters
from day one.

Now, without her
I am decidedly
alone.

A car creeps
along the street, the driver
not troubling to hide
the fact that he's watching
who comes
      who goes
at what time
      and with whom.

When Katrin and I saw a car
like this, trolling
the neighborhood, she would
lean in, whisper, *Magpie!*
her secret name for the Stasi
informants who steal
scraps of people's day-to-day
stories, collect bits
of anything that catches
their attention.

I loved the thrill
of Katrin's daring, yet
part of me was terrified
of the watchers' power.

Now, I'm less afraid
and more weary.

Weary of keeping up
my guard.

Weary of having no one
to trust, no one to share
my dreams and secrets.

Weary even
of the need for keeping
those secrets.

I drag myself through the remainder
of the day, wander
from bedroom to kitchen
      open cupboards
close them again
without finding
      without knowing
what I was looking for.

My piano whispers
from the living room
but I sidle past it
gaze averted
and sink onto my bed.

Up again.

Kitchen
      bedroom
living room
for a staring match
with eighty-eight
black and white eyes.

      I know better than to fight
      my instincts. As I play

weight slips
from my shoulders
falls away
like layers of heavy winter
clothing stripped off
until a spring breeze
caresses my skin, and

I can
      breathe
again.

Christoph arrives at our door late
Thursday evening. He and Papa
share hushed and hurried

words. Christoph's punctuating laughter
is absent. I miss details
but snippets
are enough

      a demonstration
           protesting election fraud

      arrests

      police
      brutality

and an urgent need
to get the word out.

The next morning, Christoph's news
still hangs in the air. Breakfast is a quiet
affair, all of us lost in our thoughts.

When Papa faces his students today, I doubt
he'll go so far as to criticize the police actions
        but it's likely
his students are in for a discussion
about free and fair elections.

Mama's anxious glances in his direction
tell me she's thinking exactly the same thing.

After Saturday morning school
I head downtown rather than home
to an empty apartment—Mama
is working a shift
at the department store
and Papa rarely gets home
before two.

The sun shines more brightly
than necessary, and I squint
against it, relieved
to finally board the crowded tram
        claim a seat
and lose myself
in the clatter and hum.

A woman's voice
utters the name

        Honecker

and memories of afternoons
spent with Katrin
        our *on-and-off* game
wash over me, a deluge
that somehow is both
wonderful
        and awful.

I'm lost in nostalgia
until another voice
      low and melodious
speaks my name.

I glance toward the sound, my gaze
landing on Lucas
      his arm in the air to catch
my attention, and a grin
on his face. I can't help
but smile back.

He makes his way down the aisle
as the tram
      sways. I scoot closer
to the window to make room.

You don't mind? he asks
gesturing at the space
beside me.

No.

He sinks onto the seat
and without preamble
launches into the one thing
we have in common.

I heard you play, he says.
*At Herr Weber's, as I was
leaving. You're very good.*

Herr Weber wouldn't agree,
I say. *Not that day.*

*Some days are like that.
The music just isn't there.*

It's always there, I say
noticing the disagreeable edge
in my own voice. I work to soften
it. *Some days finding it*
is more difficult.

We bump along in silence
as the tram empties
and refills a few
passengers at a time.

You're right, he says
finally, brow furrowed
in thought. *It's not the absence*
of music that makes our fingers stumble
on the keys but the presence
of distraction or pain or grief.

His serious tone
strikes me as funny
and I can't help but smirk.

Took you a while to
come up with that.

His face relaxes. He shifts
and his arm brushes mine.

I'm right, though, aren't I? he says.
At the times we most need music
we're unable to find it.

I always play the piano
when I'm upset. I really don't mean
to be contrary, but I press on.
When I'm angry, I play a little Prokofiev
and the anger finds its way out

through my fingers. Rather too loudly
at times, according to Frau Richter
next door.

And for sorrow?

Beethoven, maybe.

His eyes close and his head bobs
the slightest bit—a gentle
silent beat, as if
he might be listening
to a few measures
of *Moonlight Sonata.*

Yes, he says. *Definitely.*
Good choices. And for stress?
For lifting the weight of living
under watchful eyes?

My head jerks around, thoughts thrown
from musical meanderings.

There's no weight, I say, instantly
wary. But even as the words
leave my lips, my cheeks flame

with the lie. I shoot a furtive glance
at the woman behind us
        —was she listening?

Lucas leans in
and whispers. *Debussy,*

he says. *Always Debussy*
when I grow weary
of keeping my opinions

in a tidy, appropriate
        row.

He settles against the seat back.
From the corner of my eye
I see his face still turned
toward me. I refuse
to look at him
        this dangerous
        young man
I barely know.

Yet somehow, I can imagine
the grin he's surely aiming
in my direction.

Monday morning, Mama urges
Papa not to attend
tonight's demonstration, worried
that without the watchful eye
of Western media
the Stasi will seize
the opportunity to clamp
down on participants.

I'm a schoolteacher
going to a prayer meeting,
Papa says. *What possible problem*
could they have with me?

Mama clucks her tongue
but says nothing more.

Papa knows full well
if the Stasi wish, they can invent
plenty of problems for him
but he sees that as all the more
reason to work for change.

Freie Wahlen, he says.
Redefreiheit.

    Free elections.
    Freedom of speech.

He kisses Mama before leaving
for work.

I will not
give up, he says.

Not like Mama.

Mama thinks dreaming is a waste
of time, robbing us
of contentment. She may be willing
to settle for what *is*
rather than risk
for what could be
but to her dismay, I've always been
more like Papa.

When Herr Weber urges me
to practice, to do my best, to become
the best pianist my talent
allows for, is he not encouraging
me to dream? To see possibility
where now there are failings
      limitations
      wrong notes
      and fingers
            that barely reach
            an octave.

If I'm allowed
      at the piano
to imagine something different
      something better
emerging from the work
that comes of wanting
and dreaming
I can't help but imagine it
beyond
the piano.

Nikolaikirche: 11 September

Security forces like fence rails
stretch across every street
leading to my courtyard.
Nevertheless, the crowd
grows, determined
to march.

Stasi break through the human fence
wolves pushing their way
into pasture, snatching
people from the crowd
forcing them into police wagons.

Those who remain cry out
for reform, undaunted
by the Stasi's insatiable
hunger for control.

I arrive at Herr Weber's, find Lucas
sitting on the doorstep.

Your lesson's already
finished? I ask.

No, he says. *Herr Weber*
—he's not here.
He was
              arrested.

He tells me Frau Weber
met him at the door
when he arrived

pulling on a cardigan
as she stepped outside
hurrying away
              hoping
to find more information
about her husband.

He went out to march
in last night's demonstration,
Lucas says. *And*
he didn't come home.

I sink to the step
beside Lucas.

What sort of world is it
when a music teacher
              —an old man
can be seen
as a threat?

Herr Weber once told me
if I was going to be
a conductor, I would need
to immerse myself

in music. I didn't need convincing.

Since then, he's taken it
upon himself to expand
my musical education
sharing recordings with me
on a regular basis

Italian operas

Russian folk songs

symphonies galore

and a surprising array
of modern Western musicians

>Kristofferson
>Simon
>Dylan
>Springsteen

which he advises me to keep
to myself.

Whenever I return
a recording, he waits
>expectant
>eager
for my reaction—not
Did you like it? But
did I notice the unusual structure

of one, the intricate harmonies
of another. Did I recognize
the change in tempo here, feel
the subtle shift in mood there.

When I've missed
something important
he sends me home
with the same recording
to immerse myself

once again. I can't always hear
what Herr Weber hears
but never am I more
alive
than in the moments I rise
freshly baptized
with song.

Lucas and I decide to walk home
from Herr Weber's. It'll be an hour's walk
to my neighborhood, and another quarter
of an hour to his, but the sun is warm
on our backs, shadows stretching out
before us. Lucas and I don't talk
about what may become
of Herr Weber. For a time
we don't talk at all, lost
in the rhythm of our steps.

After a few blocks, the ease
of our silence gives way
to questions. How did Lucas
happen upon the rare opportunity
to study with Herr Weber?

Is it so unusual, Lucas says
for him to accept
a new student?

Of course it is. He's the best
teacher in the city.

Lucas shrugs
            pushes tousled hair
off his forehead. *I guess*
I'm just lucky.

Lucky? About the timing
maybe, but not about Herr Weber
accepting him. *You must be good*
for him to take you on
at this point.

I'm out of practice, he says.
*Eighteen months is a long time
away from the piano.*

Eighteen months?
My steps slow, waiting
for Lucas to say more.

Military training, he says.
*I wanted to opt out
as a pacifist, but my father
wouldn't have it. Payback
for me refusing to join
the FDJ when I was younger.
No doubt he hoped
it would repair the damage
I'd done to the family's standing
with the Party.*

But eighteen months, I say.
*You had to give up piano for
eighteen months?*

I can't imagine music
being taken from me
            no way to process
                        my thoughts, express
            my emotions. *How
did you survive?*

What do you think? he says
with a chuckle. *I was miserable
for a year and a half.*

66

Lucas and I speak mostly of music

surely there is no harm
in that

and the long walk
passes quickly. My steps
are light. So often I'm burdened
by the need to tamp down
my passion
make myself more
acceptable, but being myself
is as easy
with this boy
this stranger
as it is with Katrin.

A sharp pang stabs
puncturing the pleasant
meanderings. By the time
I say goodbye, fish
for my key, let myself
into the apartment
I'm aching
with sadness.

As I close the door behind me
the smell of pork sausages
sizzling on the stove
jars me, jostling my emotions
setting me firmly back
in the here and now. The pain
of missing Katrin sinks
into place beside my heart
while a haze drops
over the hour spent with Lucas, as if
it were a distant memory
           as if
it belongs
in someone else's life.

Herr Weber
           arrested
perhaps still in prison
stuck in a cell
or simply
gone.

This is my world.

It was foolish to speak freely
with Lucas. Just because we both require
music as much as oxygen
doesn't change the fact

he's a stranger
           not
to be trusted.

Katrin disappears
and here he is, stepping
into a coveted timeslot
with Herr Weber. Is it coincidence
that a mere two weeks later
Herr Weber is targeted
by the Stasi?

I am accustomed to living
as though there are eyes
everywhere, informants lurking

in each corner of life
but I long to trust
that sometimes people

are just people
and sometimes
relationships are real.

Even as my head argues
for the need to keep up
my guard, the sense of connection
I had with Lucas
        lingers
like a soft refrain echoing
in my heart.

Nikolaikirche: 14 September

They've posted a list
in one of my windows:
the names
of those imprisoned.

A young conscript stands
before the glass
reading and re-reading
comrades who could easily be neighbors
or even family
taken
for daring to believe
our beloved country could be *more*.

Rain soaks his shoulders and flows
down my panes.

On school days, Papa leaves
the apartment before I do.
This morning, he heads out the door
with the usual spring
in his step, still so pleased
to go to work
        to teach
after all these years.

I make my way to the Oberschule
with somewhat less
enthusiasm. Rising

when Frau Stein arrives, I greet her
in unison with the other pupils
        all of us under the watchful eye
of Herr Honecker staring
down at us from his portrait
on the classroom wall.
He needn't worry
—Frau Stein will happily inform
the State of any students
who step out of line. I imagine

Papa in his school
across town. Unlike Frau Stein
Papa does not mind his students expressing
deviant opinions in his class. Instead
it's more likely
he's surreptitiously
        encouraging
independent thought.

What kind of teacher am I,
I once heard him ask Mama,
*if I don't teach them
how to think?*

I wonder, though.
Does he know
where to draw the line?

How many tales
can his students tell at home
before a parent decides
they have a duty
to report him?

I return my attention
to Frau Stein, to the expectation
of my cooperation.
     My compliance.
The purpose of my education
has always been to awaken
my *socialist consciousness*
to mold me
into a fine, socialist citizen.

Growing up with a father
like Papa, I've always known
there are other possibilities
—different ways of seeing
and of living
in our beloved Germany.

Papa believes that we
          the people
can effect change.

I remember one night last year
when Christoph had joined us
for dinner, I questioned Papa
          struggling
to reconcile

how he could say
he loved the GDR
and yet seem to hate it
at the same time.

I do love it, he said.
*I don't want a different
country—just a better
version of this one.*

But that would make it
a different country,
I insisted. And then
he put it in language
I could understand.

Activism shapes a country,
he said, *much the same way*
you might shape a piece of music

taking a familiar melody
and re-writing it
altering the arrangement
          the tempo
                    the expression
until a dirge
becomes a hymn of praise
and an old tune
is transformed into
an anthem.

I hope he's right, but for now
all I know is that the true songs
of my heart
          what I believe
          think
          dream
must never be sung
at school.

I head home at noon
on Saturday, finished
my half-day at school.

Someone stands near the entrance
of my building, back pressed
into the cinder block
wall, head bowed
over a book.

Lucas.

The sight brings a thrill
of delight, quickly tempered
by questions.

Why is he here?
    Is it odd
that he's here?
    What does he want?
And why am I so glad
to see him?

He glances from his book
as I approach. Straightens up.

He's back, Lucas says.
Herr Weber—he's home
again.

My bubble of questions
pops, vanishing
as images rush in.
Stasi officers pulling Herr Weber
from the crowd, shoving him
into a cold dark cell.

Shari Green

He's okay?

Lucas nods. *He was
with a student
when I stopped by.*

With a student. As if
things were normal.
As if it was nothing to him
to be singled out
by the Stasi. As if
it was not terrifying.

Lucas's voice drifts
into my thoughts
        a walk—would I maybe like
        to walk
and yes, I maybe would
but then
        that damn voice
in my head

the voice that sounds like a cross
between my mother and the embodiment
of a lifetime's worth of socialist propaganda

        that voice

hisses
a warning:
he's not to be trusted.

I need to practice, I say
and silently curse
the necessity of suspicion.

Right now?

77

Already I regret
my hesitation. A walk
is just a walk. What harm
could come of it?
A walk doesn't mean
I'm letting down my guard.

You know I have to, I say. *But
how about we meet
after dinner?*

Scales
and more
scales

Mozart
and more
Mozart

then I zip
through the Haydn sonata
pushing the limits
of *allegro.*

I breathe

slow down

begin

again.

My fingers
        race ahead
stubbornly joyful.

After Haydn, I stumble
through a nocturne
        though if I'm honest
        it's not much worse
        than I usually do with Chopin.

When I'm done with the pieces
for my lesson, my hands wander
over the keys, random chords
and bits of melodies, until a song
takes shape
                as light

and cheerful
as a spring morning. I grin
like when I first heard it
coming from the speaker
of Katrin's cassette player

Here Comes the Sun.

It's a wonderful thing
how a particular pattern
of notes can lift hearts
and stir memories.

The street is quiet
as I step out
the door of my apartment block
into the cool air
of early evening.

I angle across the road
glance at a parked car
catch the eye
of the middle-aged man
in the driver's seat.

I look away.

If he's waiting for someone
it isn't me.
If he's watching someone, surely
it isn't me.

Beyond our shared love
of music, I know nothing
about Lucas. As we stroll
through the neighborhood
we exchange safe questions
     offer safe answers.

Me: *I'm an only child.*

          Him: *One brother—married.*
          Lives in Berlin.

Me: *Preparing*
for the Abitur.

          Him: *Working at Schrebers*
          as a waiter, biding my time.

Until?

What do you want, Helena? he says
ignoring my question. *Tell me*
about your plans.
Your dreams.

My neck stiffens.

Come on, he presses. *We all have dreams.*
What's life without dreams?

I could gloss over the topic
change keys midway through
this conversation, but
I simply don't want to. To speak
of dreams is to give them
substance.

I check the lock
inside me, sealing away
the sort of dreams that aren't meant
to see the light of day

but my other dreams
        the possible ones
that have already become plans
welcome the chance
to venture into fresh air.

I want to study conducting
at the Hochschule für Musik.

It's easy to share this
with Lucas, who will no doubt believe
my goal is worthwhile.
And yet I must tug a little
to free my next words.

I've wanted to be a conductor
since I was little.

I feel suddenly bare
like I've thrown off
my armor before I'm sure
whether I'm facing friend
or foe.

Brilliant, Lucas says.
You'll be great at that.

It's what Katrin would've said.
What she always said.
I don't like that I need
to hear it, but dreams
are slippery things. When I'm losing

my grip, it does my heart good
to know someone else believes
I should hold on.

A few drops of rain speckle
the sidewalk, and a memory
transports me: Years ago
in early spring, Katrin and I
collecting recyclables
after a rainfall, doing our socialist duty
and making a little pocket change
at the same time. Pale green leaves
　　　　　soaked from the downpour
dripped a gentle rhythm on the damp
sidewalks. The staccato call
of a lone blackbird
pierced the morning
and suddenly a whole chorus
of birds took up the song.

Isn't it amazing? I said to Katrin.

She shrugged, but oh
it *was* amazing, the dips and rises
　　　　　the unintended harmonies
floating in the air. I'll never forget
it. I dropped my stack
of newspapers, tipped my face toward
the high branches, waved my arms
as if conducting the birdsong.

When their voices died away
I scooped up the papers
the bottom ones now sodden.

Someday, I said, *I'll be a real conductor.*
I'll stand in the Gewandhaus and—

And conduct a whole symphony
of blackbirds?

Yes! Violins and flutes and cellos and
blackbirds. I will—you'll see.

Katrin grinned at me.
I know you will.

Now, Lucas asks which composers
are my favorite
        which is not
as simple a question
as one might think.

He makes it easier.
What music brings you
the most joy?

The question itself
lightens my heart.
Although an answer springs
to my lips
I hold it back
        savoring
how even the memory
of this music evokes in me
an expansive sense

of contentment.

Mozart? Lucas suggests, interrupting
my reverie.

Mozart is amazing, I say. *Mozart*
is the music of heaven.
And Beethoven? Beethoven is—

The music of hell?

I stop in the middle
of the sidewalk. *You don't like Beethoven?*

Lucas turns to face me
and shrugs. *His music*
depresses me.

That's because Beethoven
understands how hard
life is.

He raises his eyebrows
    skeptical.
Okay, he concedes.
What about Bach?

My gaze drifts from Lucas
up past the linden trees
    in the direction
    of the Thomaskirche
imagining
how the lingering strains of an aria
might brush the surface
of its bell tower, revealing
the beauty hidden beneath a layer
of coal-dust grime.

Bach tells us it all matters,
I say. *The pain as much*
as the joy.

Words gather, rising
within me. I've already said more
than the girls at school ever want to hear
of my opinions about classical composers
but I can't help myself.

We need to know we matter,
I say. *Bach's music*
tells me that better than anything
else I know. It elevates
life. It's like—

I breathe in, wait
for the mist of meaning
to shape itself
into words.

*It's like his music
opens a pathway
between the human
and the divine.*

Lucas is quiet. In the distance
a car door slams.

So, he says. *Not a fan
of Bach.*

His words break
some kind of spell
and I laugh.

Okay, fine, I say.
*I like Bach.
A lot.*

The breeze bears the refreshing
promise of more rain
as silence settles gently
once again.

Katrin has been falling in love
with boys since she was twelve
years old and Simon Hoffman
borrowed her pencil and blushed
when he handed it back.

She would say I'm falling
for Lucas, would say
it's about time I took
an interest.

But what I really want to know
is how long it takes
to be sure you can trust
someone enough
to even consider

     falling.

Lucas and I pause
at the intersection
kitty-corner to my building
say goodnight
    the words between us
    awkward
    for the first time.
Then he turns right
while I head left
across the road. I pull open

the door to my apartment block
glance back

    I'll wave
    if he's looking

but my grin turns
to stone, breath sticks
in my throat.

The car from earlier
is still there.

In the fading light, the glowing
tip of a cigarette confirms
the man
is still
watching.

My gut roils, unsettled
by this manifestation
of the all-seeing nature
of our government.
I stumble into the apartment
lock the door behind

me. When Mama and Papa look
up to greet me, their expressions
instantly shift to frowns
and furrowed brows
of concern. I tell them
about the magpie man.

Papa nods
as if this news
is not news
at all.

They're watching Christoph too,
he says. *Don't worry, Mäuschen.*
They have nothing more
than suspicions
about our meetings.

I gape, incredulous.
And being watched
doesn't bother you?

I despise it, he says.
But I'm careful.

I swallow my discomfort.
Even if it wasn't Papa
they were watching
        if it were Lucas
        or me

or a neighbor
I barely know
I would feel the same.
The idea of our quiet lives
feeding the Party's hunger
for information
sickens me.

Young or old
musician
teacher
shopkeeper
we are all potential
rebels
in their eyes

problems
to be controlled

or eliminated.

Disquiet stirs within me
     a vine
spreading, spindly fingers

taking hold. It's been a month
since the Vogels willingly abandoned
life in Leipzig

no doubt deciding
enough
       was enough.

Was it the restriction on travel
that forced their hand?
Or perhaps the last election—
     Papa said even Party members
were among those who became
         disillusioned
this summer when proof
emerged documenting the fraud
    —ballots missing, results
    falsified.

What line
had the government
crossed? And where is the line
for me?

What is my   *enough?*

Nikolaikirche: 17 September

They come with determined steps, faces
sad afraid angry
all at once, flowers
in their hands.

I open my arms
receive their hopes
and remembrances, the ground
along my stone walls
becoming a garden
shouting in the ears of the Stasi
the truth:

restraining people in prisons
and behind walls
will not silence
their voices.

Tonight's demonstration
was larger, Papa says
after arriving home
from the march that followed
this week's Friedensgebete

     —the peace prayers
     at Nikolaikirche.

But thankfully, he says, *it seemed
there were fewer arrests.*

Papa describes the somber tone
in the sanctuary as Pastor Führer
read aloud the names
of those still imprisoned
and called the people
to remain committed
to nonviolence. Mama listens

worry written in creases
between her brows.

When Papa speaks of the need
to carry on despite the potential
gravity of consequences
Mama interrupts.

Do you hear yourself? she says
     her voice thick.
Consequences   *matter.*

Papa's face softens. *Of course
they matter,* he says
his words wrapped
in compassion. *But justice
matters more.*

What justice was there
for Werner? For any
like him?

On the rare occasion Mama speaks
of her uncle Werner, it's with
      clipped phrases
      and hushed tones
as if
after all these years
his name still perks the ears
of the Stasi.

Perhaps it does.

I'm perched on the sofa
in the foyer when Lucas
emerges from the studio.

Although I'm anxious
to see Herr Weber
part of me hopes
he'll take his time transitioning
from Lucas's lesson
to mine

but he beckons me
into the studio
allowing Lucas and me only
a moment
for a passing *hello.*

As I close the door
behind me, thoughts of Lucas
vanish, replaced with a rush
of questions that erupt
before I've taken my place
at the piano. It's a mark
of our years together
as teacher and student
that he indulges my questions
            and perhaps that I even dare
to ask them.

Are you okay? Why
were you at the march? What
did you do
to get arrested? Why did they target
you?

Why an old music teacher
    a man retired
from the university
    a man who moves slowly
and speaks softly?

He studies me
    then sighs
settles in his chair
beside the piano.

Because, Helena, music
has power—power to change
hearts and minds, power
to bring people together
and incite boldness.
The Stasi fear everything
that gives such power
to the people.

But it was a protest, I say.
Not a revolution.

In their minds
there is no difference.

He shifts in his seat
slowly, as if his bones
ache. I study him
wanting to know more
to understand more
but the weariness etched
on his face gives me pause.

Were there always so many lines
around his eyes?

He gestures toward the piano.

Play, Helena, he says. *My heart needs music.*

It's not only Bach who speaks
to my soul, not only the German
master composers who make my spirit
sing. I crave music

that moves my feet as well
as that which moves my heart.
I need
       all of it.
All of it
is important and brilliant
and necessary

nursery songs
       and jump rope rhymes
Beethoven
       and Bruce Springsteen
even the punk bands I long to hear play
       in the dingy Ratskeller
       on Saturdays.

It's all vital, and it's all
fantastic.

The recordings Herr Weber
shares with me
and the static-laced tunes
of Western radio
are not enough.

I understand Herr Weber's words
—that music
is powerful.
       It's this power
that whispers to me
in dreams and wonderings
knitting together hopes

that likely have
no future. I've never known
anyone to set off at will, following
their heart, chasing
the music.

It simply isn't done.

Still, I can't help but be
me—dreamer
of improbable dreams.

And so, over the years
strands of hopes
      imaginings
          and what-ifs
have woven together
into the gossamer fabric
of a dream.

I should cast it aside
but instead, I allow it
to settle on my shoulders
light as a breeze.
I wear it without fail
day by day, ends tucked safely
in my breast pocket.

Now, I adjust my position
on the piano bench, focus
on the score in front of me.

A breath

      and the sonata emerges
pulled directly
from my soul.

Papa's group of friends
gathering in our home
            grows
people trickling in
one after the other.
Some carry props
in the event they must fabricate
a story

            a clarinet
            sheet music
            an empty violin case

and they greet Papa
with a significant nod
confirming the presence
of the watcher.

I hover on the fringe
listening. Mama stands, back
against the wall, casting frequent glances
at the door as if
            at any moment
the Stasi will break it down.

The seats in our small living room fill
—including the kitchen chairs
crammed into corners.
Stragglers must sit on the floor.

Papa turns on a recording
of violin concertos
            volume up
            covering voices.
Then he lays out plans
to raise money for the fines
of those imprisoned.

Christoph reports on the phone lines
now set up
in the Markuskirche office
volunteers still needed
        to contact other groups
throughout the German Democratic
Republic
        to reach out
to international media
alerting them
of police brutality suffered
by protestors.

We must get the word out,
Christoph says, pacing
as those on the floor quickly draw
in their feet. *To bolster our cause.*
To put pressure
on our government.
To let the Volkspolizei
and the Stasi know

        the world is watching.

I wonder if they might allow
a sixteen-year-old girl
to help make their illegal
phone calls.

Mama can read the thought
as easily as if it were written
on my face and shoos me
from the room.

My walks with Lucas have become
more frequent, our conversations
deeper. Now, the fading
light gives me courage
enough to share my impossible dream.

If I could do anything,
my mouse-voice confides,
I would travel.

A large chestnut leaf flutters
to the sidewalk
       golden.

I want to visit places of musical
significance. Places where music
changed everything.

So you're infected, Lucas says.

I look up
       confused
and he grins.

You've got a bad case
of musical Wanderlust.

My lips press together

      —is he making fun
    of me?

You think it's strange, I say.

Not at all. Wanderlust
is a brilliant ache
to be burdened with.

He's exactly right—it's the best
and the worst
simply because the dream I savor
in the very depths of my soul will never
be more than a desperate longing.

I cast around for a change
in subject, but Lucas pulls
the conversation right back.

Where will you go? he asks.

   Not
      where *would* I go, if
      things were different
   but
      where *will* I go.

The subtle difference sparks the desire
to give voice
   to my dream
to feel the wildness that comes
of revealing secrets.

Thanks to Herr Weber's habit
of sharing bits of history
   stories
to go with the recordings
he slips into my hands
after lessons, I know exactly
where I want to go.

I want to travel to Italy
and experience La bohème
in the Teatro Massimo

visit England
and belt out the lyrics
of The Beatles

fly to America and dance
in the field at Woodstock
   feel the passion
of their protest songs.

I spill it all before my courage
              falters
then wait for his response, heart
in my throat.

Brilliant, he says
in what seems to be a classic
Lucas response
              at least as far as dreams
              are concerned.
A wave of relief rushes
through me, leaving in its wake
clarity:
              Lucas is exactly
who I'd hoped
he was. We pause

on the sidewalk
evening light reflecting
in windowpanes, gilding
the world. He catches my hand
in his, enfolds me

in his gaze. *You're really*— he begins
but I lean in
on tiptoe, press my lips
              to his

quick
but not too quick.

As I settle back on my heels
his eyelids flutter open.
He shakes his head
chuckles
as we start
walking again.

Something, he says, giving
my hand a gentle squeeze
before letting go.
You're really quite
something.

We round a corner, and I tug
my sleeves over my hands
as a chill autumn breeze
dances between the apartment blocks
rising to frame the quiet
cobblestone street.

After your travels, Lucas says.
What will you do then?

Then? After the dream
becomes reality
      re-shapes me
           merges with
                my bones
                my spirit
          changing me
     forever
before settling into
memory?

I'll come home, I say.

I'll come home, and I'll study
piano and conducting
at the university.
      And some day
I'll raise my baton
like a wand and cast
the power of music
into the hearts
and dreams
of others.

I've always thought
there were two types
of dreams—

dreams born in darkness
nurtured, watered, fed
until they sprout
and grow into plans
for the future

and dreams
            impossible ones
that forever will remain
buried.

But now I wonder
if impossible dreams
can push upward and thrive

if only we dare
to believe.

Nikolaikirche: 21 September

The remembrance of war
is etched upon my stones.
I've seen the depths
to which humankind will stoop
in the pursuit of power.

Tonight, though, I bear witness
to compassion and fierce determination
as people step forward
in the silent dark
calling to mind the imprisoned
as they place candles
on the ground.

The light dances
across my scars
recasting them
as hope.

Friday afternoon is warm
and bright. Sweat beads
my forehead by the time I near
my apartment after school.

Before I reach the door, a man steps
from the shadows.

Fräulein, he says, stopping
my heart. *A moment.*

Against my better judgment
I turn toward him, taking care
to arrange my expression
to reflect innocence
even though I've done
nothing wrong.

The man is tall, like Papa
but stockier, his brown hair
receding. He shifts
and the sun glints
off wire-rim glasses.

I believe you are acquainted,
he says, *with Lucas
Schumacher.*

A cacophony of thoughts rages.

I knew
I shouldn't trust Lucas.

What did I
tell him?

Was it enough
to get me in trouble? To make them think
I plan to leave
like Katrin?

Enough
to put my family at risk?

But it was nothing
more than dreams.

It was foolish
to trust.

No.

I'm leaping
to conclusions.
I don't even know
what this stranger wants.

Breathe.

Just

breathe.

The man does not need me
to confirm or deny my acquaintance
with Lucas—of that I'm certain
so I simply wait for him to continue.

We have reason to be interested
in young Herr Schumacher.

Interested
in Lucas?

My gut twists with the sudden realization
that I had it all

wrong. It's not that Lucas
has been an informant
                reporting me
                betraying me
but that the Stasi
wish to make an informant
of *me.*

            Pay attention
to his plans, the man says.
Take note . . .

His words run together
                seep
into my mind
as if through a fog

damp   and gray

with a disorienting sense
            of the surreal.

Fräulein Kühn, he says, snapping
the situation into sharp focus. *If you wish*
to be admitted to university
in the future, I will expect your cooperation
now.

My mouth opens
but words
fail me.

Before Herr Weber's stories
and the world's music
planted the seed
of a dream
      deep
            deep
within me, the policies
of my government and their tight-fisted
approach to travel visas
had already ensured
such a dream would be kept firmly
in the realm of the impossible.

But my plans to study
to one day stand
      before an orchestra
have always remained
within reach

      as long as I follow
the rules, play
the part, hold
my tongue.

But now—

they threaten to take
even
      the possible
from me.

There's no way I can
be an informant. The idea
is outrageous.

When I was a young child
at school, my teacher
explained our duty
as good socialist citizens
to inform on any classmates
whose words or actions
might be deemed

inappropriate. I couldn't rat out others
back then, no matter how many lessons
I heard on *duty*

and I can't imagine doing it
now.
          But surely
they can't withhold
the one thing I believe
I was made for.

Cold truth hisses
in my ear:

they most certainly
can
          and they will.

I could simply tell Lucas
and become of no use
as an informant

          but they could retaliate
and take

everything.

I could tell Lucas and pretend
to cooperate with the Stasi
hand-feed them
empty words and lies

but

would Lucas ever fully
trust me?

The only way to hold on
to both Lucas and my dreams
is to carry this secret

      act
as if things are fine

and when the Stasi
come calling, offer them

           nothing
no matter
what I may have learned.

Even with my decision made
I lie awake long
into the night.

Nikolaikirche: 25 September

Troops surround my courtyard
ringing the gathered citizens
as if a chain of human arms
will contain the masses
when those inside pour forth
from the sanctuary.
Stasi fall into place
behind the security forces, armed
with guns and dogs.

Inside, Pastor Wonneberger preaches
blessed are the peacemakers
urges nonviolence
speaks of confronting fears.
The Stasi, he says, are paper
tigers.

Music signals the end
of the service, the beginning
of the march, voices and spirits
rising, resolve strengthening.

Outside, the crowd shifts its weight
police fortify their posture
Stasi officers tighten
their grip on weapons, everyone
watching, waiting
for my doors to swing
open and the march to begin.
The protestors are hemmed in
latecomers barricaded from joining
little space for churchgoers
to exit, let alone join
the demonstration.

I can only hope
as final prayers break free and soar
beyond my vaulted ceiling
that this night will not end
with the cobblestones
of my courtyard bathed in blood.

Papa bursts into the apartment
after the march, his face radiant.

It was amazing! he tells Mama.
*The police had people ringed in
outside the church.*

Mama sucks in her breath
but Papa continues.
*When those of us inside
joined their ranks, we were singing*
We Shall Overcome—*it took me back.
Remember, Maria?*

He hugs her, and Mama's breath eases
out. When Papa steps back
a soft smile graces Mama's face
and her gaze shifts, loses
focus as if looking back in time.

I feel a distinct twinge
like I'm being left out
of a wonderful secret.

A song from when you were young? I ask
nudging their attention back
to the present.

I'm still young, Mäuschen, says Papa
with a wink. *But yes, Mama and I sang
that song when we were only a little
older than you. Reverend King,
from America, visited Berlin.*

I can't imagine Mama having anything
to do with demonstrations now
or then. My mind's eye flits

to the burgundy photo
album, snapshots stuck to cream-
colored pages telling stories
of my parents' college years
in Berlin, their wedding, the move
to Leipzig, a faded color
portrait of my mother
      round-bellied
fastened to the last page.
I make my appearance
on the first page
of a blue album, a new chapter
in our family story.

But it's tonight's story
I want to hear. *What
does a visiting preacher have to do
with an old song?*

Everything, Papa says.
*All those years ago in Berlin
we went to hear him preach.
Such a crowd! He spoke of freedom
     reconciliation
        breaking down walls
            of hostility.*

I smirk, now skeptical.
*You still remember a sermon
from years ago?*

Some things, he says,
you never forget.

Papa recounts the contagious passion
of the American, even as King's
words were filtered
through the passive tones
of an interpreter. *We knew*
a little of the civil rights movement
in America, Papa says
and we believed then
as now
that we too would overcome
            that we will
overcome.

The photo album images
in my memory come alive
channeling the passionate student
he must've been, the activist
for change he desires
to be now. *Next week,*

Liebchen, he says to Mama
you must come.

But tonight, she says
laughing at his earnestness.
What else happened tonight?

They sang with us. All of them
—thousands of voices. The police
surrounding us
            they stepped aside
            opened space
for us to pass through.
And we marched.
We marched past the train station
past the Reformierte Kirche
all the way
to the overpass.

Through the remainder
of the evening, Papa spontaneously
      and frequently
hums the *Overcome* song.

At first Mama shushes him
but she gives up, shaking her head
as if he's an irrepressible child.

Mama rarely betrays
any discontent
with the ways of our country
    aside from wistful memories
    of oranges
    and an occasional longing
    for real coffee.
But old photos suggest
she and Papa used to share
much more in common
    including a passion
    for justice
        peace
            freedom.

I have no memory of a mother
like that. The change

I've learned, is inextricably
linked to her father's brother—
my great-uncle
    Werner Drescher.

I've never met Mama's uncle
but I've pieced together
who he is
        —or was

writer
dissident
outspoken critic of
    the Party
    and the Stasi.

His contact
    a businessman
    visiting the GDR from the West
would carry Uncle Werner's essays
and opinion pieces, print them
in Western newspapers until
Werner disappeared
    the same year Mama and Papa
were married.

No one seems to know
if he was killed by the State
or if he languished

    (languishes still)

in a lonely prison
        cell.

A quick hello
in the foyer
between

our lessons

    a kiss
barely brushing soft
lips

    a promise
to meet tomorrow.

When I step into the studio
Herr Weber extends
a large brown envelope
says, *I received this*
in yesterday's post.

I turn over the slim envelope
look for a clue
as to why he's sharing
this with me, glance at the top
corner for a return address.
It's blank, but the postmark
says *Frankfurt.*

I raise my eyebrows and he nods
toward the envelope, indicating I should
open it. I slip out the single sheet
of music notation paper, scan
the handwritten score.

Bach's *Bourrée in E Minor.*

My gaze slides quickly
across the notes dancing along
three staves, melody playing
in my mind, familiar
measures above, but a different
tune emerging below

on the bottom staff.
            Perhaps complementary
at least a little, but the timing
is all wrong.

The longer I listen, the clearer
it becomes that the melody
on the third

staff does not belong
in the *Bourrée.*

My pulse quickens, heart
understanding even before
my thoughts have fully formed.

But no. It couldn't be.

I glance at Herr Weber. *What is this?*
The beginnings of two songs
on one score
errors in both, and not at all
blended. It makes

no sense.

Herr Weber chuckles. *Notation*
was never her strong suit.

His eyes sparkle, as if he knows
something I don't

except maybe

I *do.*

Who sent this to you? I ask, the page
trembling
in my hands.

Not to me. He leans forward, nudging
his glasses up his nose.
He taps the top of the page.

In small letters
beneath the careful black ink-
strokes of the title
is a dedication—
      not something Bach
      was wont to do:
for the conductor.

Doubt
vanishes.

I hear Katrin's voice calling
me *the conductor*

see us huddled beneath a quilt
listening to The Beatles
memorizing melodies and lyrics
song after song, including
Blackbird—which only hints
at a suggestion of *Bourrée*
in E Minor.

I know
who wrote this mismatched
blend of Bach and The Beatles

and I know it was written
for me.

Trust Katrin
to mash up
two songs I love
into a barely recognizable mess.

Trust Katrin
to let me know
she's safe
without giving away anything
to the Stasi snooping
through lettermail.

Trust Katrin
to tell me
she loves me
while confirming
she's gone
for good.

The black notes
on the page in my hand
blur.

In the quiet of my room
the two songs dance
in my mind, one taking the lead
for a time, until the other
emerges—a medley
of call and response
evoking memories
of recitals and contraband
cassette tapes and a friend
who believed in me

always.

I hate that the state
of things in my country
made Katrin's parents believe
their only option was to

leave
       everything

risk
       everything

and flee.

Was escape to the West
truly the best
way for them to climb
from beneath the heel
of the regime?

I trace my fingers along
the notes on the third staff.
As *Blackbird* soars again
in my head
certainty blooms
in my heart:

leaving
is not the only way
to rise.

Lucas and I meet at the park
near my school and walk
toward his place. Hearing from Katrin
all but buried thoughts of my encounter
with the Stasi, and even now
as they resurface, I'm content
with my decision to keep quiet.

A hint of color catches my eye
—pale turquoise in the shade
of a hawthorn shrub.

I stoop and retrieve
the broken bit
of a speckled egg
        a remnant
            cast off by a tiny bird
            from a spring brood.

I heard from Katrin, I say
tucking the broken shell
gently
back beneath the shrub.
My friend
        Herr Weber's student
who left
in the summer. She's okay.

I don't mention the perfect form
of Katrin's message or how
deeply her covert communication
impacted me. That part
of the truth feels as precious
as a tiny turquoise egg
and I hold it close
inside.

The Schumachers' apartment
is much like ours in layout
and furnishings, but in tone
completely different:

a State flag stands
at attention
in the living room

framed photos
        Honecker
        and Lenin
shout from the walls

and a sense of order
not often achieved
in my own home
compels me to straighten
my shoes on the mat.

Lucas is eager to share Herr Weber's
recording of the Philharmonia
Orchestra performing Williams's
*The Lark
Ascending.*

I don't mention that I know
the piece, that Papa names it
among his favorites. Instead
I close my eyes, savor
the exquisite rise
and fall of the violin.

Midway through the song
Lucas and I lose the *Lark*
and find
one another

become entangled
for a time. At the sound
of a key turning in the front
door lock, we break apart, hearts
fluttering.

Frau Schumacher's eyebrows
arch upward
      no doubt
      we are a tad disheveled
but she greets me
politely. Nevertheless

judgment pecks at my skin
setting me on edge.

Lucas plays the recording
again, and we perch
on the sofa
      still
      silent
until the final notes
sound.

Our conversation turns
to politics, earning a frown
from Lucas's mother as she crosses
through the room into the kitchen.

Lucas lowers his voice.
This week's demonstration
was even larger, he says.

I gape. *You take part*
in the marches?

I should change the subject—this is exactly
the sort of thing the Stasi will want
to know—but I crave
more, want to know everything
about him.

Sometimes, he says in response
then shakes his head.
This country
is so
broken.

A spark flares, and I imagine
            for a moment
Lucas and I at the helm
of a group like Papa's
—young people working together
to make a difference.

I hate living
here, he says, voice
laced with bitterness

and the spark
            dies.

Thousands have left,
he says. *Thousands who know*
life is better
elsewhere.

Is that what the Vogels thought?
Do they feel the same
now they've seen life
from the other side
of the wall?

      Lucas glances
at the clock, curses
softly, says
I have to go.

A shot of panic rushes
through me
      a flurry of wings
until my thoughts catch up
with my heart—of course
he's not speaking of leaving
the country.

      He simply has to get ready
for work.

That's a good thing
about living here, I say.
I've heard many in the West
are poor—homeless, even,
because there are no jobs.

I don't know about that,
he says, and as I stoop
to retrieve my shoes, I wonder
if what they tell us

is true. Is life
for people like Katrin
      and me
harder here
      or in the West?

The magpie man slides
from the shadows
as I approach. My steps
falter.

Have you anything
to tell me, Fräulein?

Nein. My voice is little more
than a squeak. I swallow hard.
We haven't much time
to talk between lessons.

He shakes a cigarette
from its package
lights it
while I stand
            silent.
He exhales a cloud
of smoke before responding.

And on your walks?

My heart screeches to a stop
then stammers
            forward. Of course
he knows about the walks.
I—no, nothing
of significance.

I don't meet his eyes, can barely breathe
beneath the crushing pressure
in my chest.

You know
what's at stake.

A memory darts in

    after a rain
        conducting
    the blackbird chorus

    Katrin
        believing
  in me
  and my plan.

My plan—my long-standing
        long-imagined
plan

    my hope and my heart

    slipping
    through my fingers.

Would Katrin have believed
in me if I were
a traitor
    informant
poor excuse
    for a friend?

I clench
    and unclench
my hands, then set my jaw
and look him
in the eye.

I have nothing
to tell you.

The man studies me, mouth pinched
cigarette now clenched
between his fingers.

Your father, he says.
*He enjoys teaching
does he not? It would be a shame
if his service
was no longer required.*

His words ricochet
in my skull. Before their impact
settles, the magpie man
vanishes, acrid smoke
from his cigarette hanging
in the air.

At the door to my apartment
I pause, hand resting
on the doorknob
     wait
for the trembling
to stop.

A breath to compose
     myself

     then I step inside.

Mama, of course, notices
immediately that something's off.
I've never been able to hide
anything of significance
from her.

The man who's been watching,
I say. *He's there again.*

Don't worry, Papa says
from the living room
where he sits surrounded
by students' papers.
He's trying to intimidate me.

I open my mouth to correct him
to let out the truth
but Mama's expression stops
my words. Turning away

from her, I reach for plates
and silverware to set the table
for dinner. If Mama knew
the truth
she'd never let me leave
the house again.

And Papa? If he knew
it was *me* the Stasi
were trying to intimidate
it would surely tempt him nearer
to outright rebellion.

After what happened
to Herr Weber for simply daring
to protest, I don't want to think
what Papa's fate could be
if he's pushed
too
        far.

If Papa couldn't teach
he would fret
over the fate of
his students

the ones
who don't fit
the socialist vision
the ones who need to believe
another way is possible.

>Who will teach them
>to think?

>Who will equip them
>to act?

Mama always warns him
—says it's one thing to allow
his students leeway to explore
ideas and quite another
for Papa to toss his own
opinions into the ring.

>*They'll throw you in prison*
>*—you know they will. Or*
>*you'll simply disappear*
>*like Werner. Then what good*
>*will you be to your students?*

I've no doubt Papa would
willingly go to prison
for his beliefs, but the thought
of being taken from his students
>and his family
has always been enough
to rein in his desire
to rebel.

I need to play. My hands
settle on the keys and the cool
smooth ivory
beneath my fingertips
soothes
like a summer day.

I'm drawn to the hymns
     Gerhardt's *Befiehl du deine Wege*
     Nicolai's *Wie schön leuchtet.*
They strengthen me
so when I finally land
on Martin Luther's *Ein feste Burg*
     —A Mighty Fortress
neither my hands
nor my heart
falter.

Here in the GDR, we may not confess
as much, but I believe
in every heart
is a longing

music
or travel

free speech and fair
        elections

a promising future

things as small
as Mama's wish
        for oranges
as significant
as justice
        for all.

We shouldn't have to live
in fear, abandon home, risk
imprisonment or
elimination
in pursuit of simple
        honest
hope.

Dreams

should be allowed

to stretch

their wings

and
g r o w

into possibilities.

October 1989

Christoph arrives Sunday afternoon
accompanied by a young couple
I don't recognize. A grim mood
sweeps into the room with them.

The woman—Brigitte
has news from the hospital
where she works.

The lab has been increasing
the quantity of blood
kept on hand, she says.
And we've been told
to have all medical staff
on standby
Monday night.

Her words are met
with silence.

Finally Papa says,
Then we must march
in such a way
as to give them no reason
for violence.

Brigitte's husband shifts
from one foot
            to the other.

The problem, he says, *is that*
the Stasi don't seem to require
a reason.

Terror
and determination
wrestle
        a wild dance
within me.

I understand Mama's fears
        —they reside also
                in me

but I am not   Mama. I'll never
believe keeping the peace
means closing my eyes to injustice, never
again be content to hold
my tongue and hope
another speaks the truth, never
be okay with a government that threatens
me
        or my Papa
                        or any
                        of our citizens.

Tomorrow
I will march.

It's true I'm uncomfortable
with crowds, true I tremble
at the thought of conflict
of making myself completely
        vulnerable

and yet
in my dreams
music transcends my fears.

If I believe I can stand
in front of an orchestra, raise

my baton, conduct
a symphony for a large audience

surely, I can stand
before a line of police officers, raise
my voice, demonstrate
surrounded by a host of allies.

Freedom

     if it can be achieved

will be a glorious
symphony.

Nikolaikirche: 2 October

They slip inside, hours early
Party members and Stasi
filling my pews
waiting stiffly or burying
their nose in Party newspapers.

Pastor Führer swallows a smirk
as he acknowledges them
but mingled curiosity and amusement
dance in his eyes.
Everyone is welcome, he says.

Eventually, the regulars arrive
churchgoers and group members
gathering, like-minded souls
hoping for change, praying
for peace.

Some who came to observe or spy
or intimidate
find themselves opening
hearts to pray. Others remain
stone-faced.
If they hoped to discourage
or discredit
those who participate week after week
they have failed.
They do not realize
swelling the numbers only serves
to encourage the people.

I rise from the piano
the persistent
    gentle
        rhythm
of Bach's *Prelude in C Major*
still pulsing
within me.

The sweet harmony
of its chord progressions
        calmed me
while I waited
for clock hands to inch
           forward
and now
its beauty and simplicity
are my lifeblood
keeping me focused and

    moving.

A passing thought slips
toward my heart, presses air
from my lungs.

In another time
I would've told Mama
I was going
to Katrin's

an easy cover story.

Now, I say I'm meeting Lucas
and leave the apartment, only
to have my lie transformed
into truth:

Lucas is meters away
walking toward me.

A grin leaps to his face
but in an instant, falls away.

You're going out? he says.

I admit my plan
to join the demonstration.

Perfect, he says, the smile
returning. *I wanted to march
but decided I'd rather see you
instead. Now we can go
together.*

Lucas attending another march
seems like one more reason
for the Stasi to press me
to share details

or risk
Papa's job.

Have I gone about this
all wrong? Perhaps I ought
to tell Lucas, spill the truth
      get it over with.
But something holds me back.

Hoping at least to keep him
from harm's way, I say
I'll go next week.
Let's just visit tonight.

But Lucas insists
we stick with my plan
says it should be really something
to see the crowds. He's heard
that tonight, a second church
is also hosting peace prayers
to accommodate the demand.

Before I know it, we're both squeezed
into a seat on the tram, heading downtown
toward the Nikolaikirche.

On foot again, Lucas and I move nearer
to the overflowing square. I wish
we'd come earlier. I'd love to be

inside the church, hearing
the prayers
    the discussion
        the reading
           of prisoners' names

but Mama would've been suspicious
if I'd tried to leave as early
as Papa.

Papa had almost convinced her
to go with him tonight, but the news
from Brigitte scared her.
        Now, a pang of guilt
jolts me—she'd be so worried
if she knew I was here.

And what if something *does* happen?
To me, or to Lucas. To Papa.

I look to Lucas
grateful for his reassuring smile
and the warmth of his hand
on the small of my back.

I stretch on tiptoe, crane to see
as the church doors open. People surge
from the building clutching candles
      and courage.

As one, we move
past Karl-Marx-Platz
and march
along the ring road.

Tension crackles
in the air. Around me
chants rise
like thunderclouds:

No violence!
Freedom
for the arrested!

Some call out
        Gorbi! Gorbi!
wishing Russia's Gorbachev
to step in and save us all.

The chorus of voices
raises in me a song
        of longing.

I want to shout
for free travel
but I remember Herr Weber
        locked up overnight
        for no good reason
        at all
remember the Vogels
        abandoning homeland
        by stealth
remember Papa, compelled
        to censor himself
and instead, I join those
who simply cry
for freedom.

        Freiheit! Freiheit!

A row of combat troops
blocks the road ahead.
My confidence
                    stumbles
but I slip in front of Lucas
shielding him
from view. I turn to face him.

They're watching you, I say
the whole truth of the magpie man
rising, ready to spill out.
We should leave.

Before I can explain
he shakes his head
holds up a hand to halt
my words. *They've been watching*

me my whole life, he says. *My refusal*
to join the Free German Youth,
my outspoken nature
in school, my participation
in these protests. He shrugs.
Even if I knew they planned
to arrest me tonight, I'd keep
marching. I won't change
my views. I'll never offer
a single word of support
for the Party.

His words
        unnerve me.
My head spins with images
of Lucas being hauled away, hurled
into a dark van, disappearing
forever.

Helena, he says
and our eyes
lock.

In that moment, I know I need
to be here with him, know
all that matters right now is this.

And then I hear it

    deep within me

the *Prelude*
    pulsing.

There comes a time
when every voice
must cry out, a time

when every person must lean
into their fear, spread their wings
and rise up.

That time
is now.

Pressure from the people weakens
the blockade. We break
through, continue marching
to Friedrich-Engels-Platz.
Here, the crowd thins,
protestors breaking away, pleased
with how far we've come.

Some talk of carrying on
to the Runde Ecke, and I know
wherever Papa is in this mass
of people, he'll be among those
who press on.

The thought of marching
to the Stasi headquarters shoots
a thrill of terror through me.
Would they let us get so far?
Could that be the tipping point

causing the night to erupt
                              with violence?

I scan the scene in vain hope
of seeing Papa. *Stay safe,*
          Papa. Stay safe.

I swallow hard over a lump of fear.
Poor Mama, waiting at home
alone.
          I should be with her.

I'm almost glad
I have an excuse to turn back
—and a way to ensure
Lucas turns back.

Let's go home.

Maybe there's safety
in numbers. Maybe they can't watch
every person of interest at the same time.
Regardless of the reason
behind our uneventful
participation, the tension
in my shoulders
eases as we make our way
to the fringes of the crowd, then to the tram
toward home.

Lucas walks me to the door
where we linger
hearts pressed together.

When we finally part
I slip inside
where Mama waits
for Papa's return.

I make a futile attempt
at homework, while Mama
paces. She pauses only to stare
at the apartment door
as if by willing it
she can make Papa appear.

At nine o'clock, she begs
for a distraction.
Play something, Helena,
she says. *Anything.*

I choose Mozart's *Serenade
in G Major*—cheerful
and uplifting
      or it would be
         if I didn't butcher it

thanks to visions of Papa
being attacked by police
and thrown in a cell.

As I stumble my way toward
the end of the piece
          the lock turns.
Mama sucks in her breath

          —he's home.

When Mama demands to know
why he's so late, Papa shrugs
with wide-eyed innocence.
We marched further, Liebchen,
he says. *It took*
> *longer.*

The worry I felt while Mama paced
dissolves, bubbling up
> spilling
> > into laughter.

What's so funny? Papa says
which only makes me laugh
harder. He smiles

but it quickly fades.
When he sinks onto the sofa
> rubs his face
takes a long breath, my worries
rush back.

We made it to the Thomaskirche,
he says. *Incredible. But then*
the police came at us.

The police
> with helmets
> shields
> weapons
> and dogs

and the protestors
> with tattered banners
> and the extinguished stubs
> > of candles.

I'm fine, he assures us. *But some
were arrested, and many more
        injured.*

It could've been Papa
attacked by police.
It could've been me
        or Lucas.
Does it matter who it was?
One person suffering violence
        or injustice
affects us all.

The moment
between our lessons
is brief

      always too brief

but today, the glance we share
and the barely there touch
of our hands is

      a pause

aptly placed in time
adding a world of meaning.

We have a history now. The risk
      and triumph
of last night's march
are woven
into our story forever.

That evening, Christoph arrives
bearing a copy of the *Volkszeitung.*

Have you seen it? he asks
extending the newspaper
to Papa, stabbing a finger
at an article on the page.
They say the police action
was necessary to maintain
                    control.

Papa scans the story
while Mama peers at it
over his shoulder.
Then he shrugs
            half-heartedly.
What else do you expect
them to say?

Christoph pulls up
his shirtsleeve, revealing
a purple slash
            stretching
along his upper arm.
I can almost feel the sting
of a police baton.

They think this was necessary,
he says, *to prevent my walking*
from getting out of control?

He shakes his head
lets his sleeve fall into place
as he and Papa launch
into discussion about freedom
of the press.

A flickering black and white image
on the television in the corner
catches my attention, and I recognize
Kurt Masur
        the great conductor.

I turn up the volume, lean in
to listen. *Papa,* I say, hoping
he and Christoph will hush
so I can hear. *One minute.*
After all the talk of violence
and protests, anything to do
with music will be a welcome change.
But Herr Masur speaks not of music
and symphonies, but of the shame
of last night's events, frankly
condemning the police
                violence.

What a fool, Mama says.

He's right, Christoph says
and Mama shakes her head.

Musicians
        artists
                writers
all have a habit of pushing limits,
she says. *They push their luck.*
We in the GDR do not have
a large supply
of luck.

I'm not sure if Herr Masur's words
were foolish
or daring

or if saying them
was simply the right thing
to do, but regardless
it took courage.

Perhaps Herr Weber was wrong.
Perhaps the power of music
isn't in the music itself
but in its ability to awaken
the power and courage
already present
within us.

News
>slams

its way into the lives
of every citizen

of the German
Democratic Republic.

Herr Honecker proclaimed
an end to visa-free
travel with Czechoslovakia.

Followed it up
with a ban on transit
>to Romania
>and Bulgaria.

The people have no way of leaving.

We are in
>a cage

and our government
has stolen
the key.

It's time, **Lucas says.** *There's no point*
in waiting.

We've paused beneath a grand
oak tree in the Auenwald park
       a world away from noise and crowds
despite being so near
the city center.

Waiting for what? I ask Lucas.

For change. Reform. Justice.
It's never going
to happen.

But the protests, I say.
Papa believes—

Lucas shakes his head, and my words
evaporate.

My brother will take me in, he says.
He'll let me stay
while I finalize details.
We won't cross in Berlin
but there's a place
south of the city.

Understanding prickles
in my chest. He's speaking
of escape.

The face of the magpie man
invades my mind, and I see him
as plain as if he'd once again slid
from the shadows. *Don't tell*

me this, I say. Unspoken:
don't tell me
anything I might be tempted
to offer in exchange
for the security
of my education. Papa's job.

My gut churns. If they know Lucas aims
to steal past armed guards
he doesn't stand a chance.

You can't go, I say. *Seriously.*
The Stasi
are watching you.

He waves away my warning
as if it were a harmless fly.

They're watching us all, Helena. They've always
been watching, and they'll always be
    watching.
We can't let that stop us. People escape
all the time. We have to be smart
about it, is all.

He continues sketching the basics
of his plan

    bicycles
    ladders
    a shed
        in a rural yard
        outside Berlin.

Please, I finally say.
Don't go. You mustn't
risk it.

But Helena—he reaches
for my hands, clasps them both
in his. My heart stumbles
with the warmth
of his skin on mine.

I want you
to come with me.

As if his touch suddenly
blazes, I yank my hands
from his grasp.

It's madness.

      I can't

don't want

—this

        is my home.

When I find my voice
it is un-
        wavering.

I've never wanted
to leave.

Confusion
          or hurt
flashes
across his face, replaced
almost instantly by a return
to childish excitement.

From the West, he says
you can go anywhere.
Abbey Road and Woodstock.
Every place
on your list.
        And your friend—
you can visit her
whenever you want.

He leans forward
          so earnest
    and nearly
          irresistible.

All your dreams, Helena
—it's the only way.

I fear he's right. Fear
there's no other way
to hold on
to hope

      for my dreams
      for my future

now that the Stasi
have set me
in their sights.

But if I leave
they will take it out
on Papa.

And if Lucas leaves
      or tries to . . .

I think of the gunshot
years ago, the news that fired
my imagination.

There may well be wonders
beyond the wall, but that boy
in the news will never see
them, nor will he ever see
home again.

It's too dangerous,
I say. *You'd be mad*
to try it.

Completely mad, he says
eyes bright
with a light that is almost
      infectious.

What's the point
of avoiding risk
if it means missing out
on life?

But this much risk?

This much risk
is too much.

Lucas's excitement nudges
at the corner of my fear
but I brace
against it, knowing
if I let down my guard
        embrace
his plan, it will overtake me
        a landslide careening
down a mountain

leaving nothing but rubble
in its wake.

I tell Lucas I need time
to think, make plans
to meet again tomorrow
but there's no question
what my answer will be.

Even if I were certain
my parents would be safe
I could not leave.

Leipzig
is in my bones

the surrounding landscape
        etched
on my soul.

The GDR
        my Germany
is part of me
as much as the music
of its most famous
composers.

To leave
would be to
tear

        my

self

        in

pieces.

The room is dismal, the only light
a dull strip from a gap
in the curtains.

I sit on the piano bench
rubbing my hands together
to warm them. The heat's out
again, the fluctuating temperature
and humidity so hard
on my piano.

      I shuffle
through sheet music
but nothing whispers
to my heart.

As I sink back down
empty-handed, my fingers
land lightly
on the keys.

      My right hand softly
      picks out a melody
      a few bars
      familiar
            but distant.

Left hand
fills in chords, the song
emerging
      strengthening
as I play verse
after verse.

The lock clicks
and I'm playing

playing still, hands and heart
united

until—

Helena!

My mother's voice, sharp
slams a door within me
and my hands leap
from the keys, clench
in front of my chest.

Mama flies
across the room. *Why
would you play that song?*

That song?

A memory
flutters through me
Papa humming this tune
eyes alight.

I stammer an apology.
I wasn't thinking.

Behind me, Mama eases out
a long breath, steadying herself
before gently grasping
my shoulders. She presses
a kiss to the top of my head.

We must always think,
she says, calm
now but leaving
no room for debate.

She moves to the kitchen
fills a kettle
to make tea, and I disappear
into my room
the melody still coursing
through my veins.

We shall overcome.

This I know:

Lucas will leave
one way or the other

     with
          or without me

     by secret escape
          or by the bullets
          of border guards

and I

     will stay.

I can't say what is right
for anyone else. I don't know
their stories. But I've listened
       to Papa and Christoph
       to Mama
       to Lucas
even to the words I imagine
            Katrin would offer

different stories, all of them
and different choices

yet one thing remains
undisputed:

a government
clutching at power
      without heed for
      justice
is failing
its people.

Perhaps there is risk
no matter what choice
we make—risk in change
and risk in staying
the same. But for me
      as for Papa
there is only one path
forward.

We
       the people
must
take a stand.

I convince Lucas
to hold off
on his plans
             for now
and march with me again
on Monday. The risk
still terrifies me

          they could snatch him away
          at any moment

but if Lucas again feels the power
of the crowds
if we march further
dare more
sense our skin tingle
with the nearness
of change

          perhaps
he'll give our country
one more chance.

Kneeling on the kitchen floor
of his apartment, we cut a strip
from the bed sheet I brought
from home
      (Mama will be furious
        when she finds out)
and we create a banner, our demand
painted in bold red letters:

     Reisefreiheit!

Freedom to travel.

True, our country needs
so much more reform
     fair elections
     care for the environment
     the right
          to free speech
but more than any of that
my heart longs for a Germany
with open borders
     especially between
     its two halves.

As Lucas and I wash dabs
of red paint from our hands
     sharing the small space
     in front of the sink

        so close
arms
     bumping

we turn
at the same moment
forget

all else
wrap one another, hands dripping
lips pressing soft together
                            water
still rushing from the faucet.

When we break apart, my thoughts
wander back to the banner
and our demand.

It's not my dream of travel
that drives my current longing

for change, but how
Reisefreiheit would negate
the need for Lucas
to entertain dangerous
thoughts of escape.

The magpie man climbs
from his car, and my stomach
clenches. The drop of red
paint on my jeans
seems to scream out
for notice, but I know
the man's not here
about a banner.

The Stasi know of our walks
know of my plans
       for the future
know of Papa's passion
       for teaching.

What if this is a test?

What if they already know
of the ladders waiting
for Lucas in the shed
outside Berlin?

If that's the case and I fail
to confess his plans
it is Papa who will pay.

But Lucas is counting on me.

How foolish I was
to think it would be easy
to lie to this man.

The knot in my belly tightens
and my mind briefly darts
away. I imagine myself retching
      spewing bile

on the shoes
of the magpie man.

He shifts.

I'm a busy man, Fräulein,
he says, an edge
to his voice. *Tell me
your information   now
          or I shall take action
to ensure you are more
cooperative.*

I stare at his shoes

          black and bile-free
          but in need of polish

and I tell him

          everything.

I have become
the very thing
I hate.

All day I lie
in bed, wrapped
in remorse
my room dim
and stuffy, window
and curtains closed
blocking
even the birdsong.

How is it that our government
declares those who flee
            traitors
when the government itself
            in its desperate need to save
            face and cling to power
beats and imprisons us
or transforms us
into the worst sort of traitors

            —not by driving us
to leave
            but by draining us
of decency. Shaping us into spies.
Setting us one
                        against the other.

            Me
                        against Lucas.

How has my country come to this?

When did Germany turn
against its own people?

Nikolaikirche: 7 October
Fortieth Anniversary of the GDR

It should be no surprise
that forced celebration
does not end well.

Blocked from their usual meeting place
in my courtyard, the people gather
in streets beyond, ten thousand
strong. The demonstration
is peaceful, but officials have decided
the only way to maintain control
is to label the protestors
as enemies.

The police strike
with water cannons
and clubs
chase down demonstrators
as they flee.

I open my arms to shelter them
but they do not come.
Perhaps they know if the Stasi
do not restrain themselves
in the sacred space of our streets

little more can be expected
within my sanctuary.

Instead, the people scatter
bodies bruised and bloodied
the whole holy world
made a forum for injustice.

It's not until late afternoon
when Papa's voice breaks through
crackling with anger
that I finally emerge.

I sidle into the living room
lurk beside the piano
thoughts of my betrayal slipping
      for a moment
into the shadows.

Two hundred arrested! Papa says
gesturing furiously. *Maybe more.*
They've got them locked up
in horse stalls
      at the fairgrounds. As if
we're animals.

Mama presses a hand
over her mouth
as Papa rages on.

There's talk
of a Tiananmen solution,
he says, his words sparking
a memory I can't quite grasp.
Honecker seems headed
in that direction—I certainly
wouldn't put it past him.

I take a step further
into the room, startling Mama.
Ignoring her attempt
to brush off the conversation
I ask, *What does it mean?*
That possible solution.

It was no solution, Papa says
jaw tense. *It was slaughter.*

And then I remember
news stories last spring
protestors
      in China
and their government choosing
to kill them
rather than seek a peaceful
resolution.

The same fire blazing in Papa
flames
in my chest.

And Herr Honecker agrees *with that?*
What kind of leader would—

Helena! Mama's eyes flash.
Keep your voice down.

I bite back my words, and they fall
burning
in my gut.

        Any leader
who doesn't value the lives
of the people
        is no leader
      at all.

I must see Lucas
must impress on him
> the truth:

thanks to me, the Stasi
will surely seize him
> or gun him down
the moment he moves
to cross the border
to the West.

> A weight
lashes itself around my neck.
He will brush off my warning.
I'm sure of it. Perhaps even take it
as a challenge, drawn
to the danger.

It's too late.
> I have sealed
> his fate.

My shame
at what I've done
> what I've become
thickens
my blood, paralyzes
my limbs.

I can't
go to him.

Sunday morning, we set off
for the worship service
at the Thomaskirche
        Mama, Papa, and me.

Papa's still agitated, anger
bubbling beneath
the surface. I'm not sure church
is where he wants to be
—it was Mama
who suggested it, perhaps hoping
Papa would find peace.

        I'm only hoping
for a little grace

a whisper

to wend its way into my heart
pry its fingers into the knot
of anger and guilt
        loosen
        its hold
so I can act.

When I'm struggling
to learn a difficult piece
of music, I break it down
examine
> complex timing
> unexpected accidentals
> hard-to-reach combinations
> > of notes
until I understand
what the song is teaching me.

Now, I examine the notes
clashing within me
> anger
> remorse
> confusion
> defiance
> fear
until I uncover a melody
that rings with a daunting
but certain
truth:

I am the conductor
and it's up to me
to shape the discordant
parts of my life
into a song of freedom.

Christoph pulls stacks of paper
from the box on our kitchen table
thrusting them into the hands
of those gathered.

We need to reach as many
as possible—churchgoers
and protesters, the Volkspolizei
and members of the Stasi.

A page flutters
        to the floor.

I scoop it up, scan
the mimeographed flyer
appealing for nonviolence
during Monday's march.

Is this all of them? Papa asks.

Not even close, Christoph says
with a hint of a grin.
Twenty-five thousand
were printed in the office
of the Lukaskirche.

Christoph holds an armful
of flyers, glances
at the already-full hands
of the people around him.

I'll take some, I say
careful not to look
in Mama's direction.

Instead, I catch Papa's eye
and he nods.

The irony
is almost funny
         sneaking
through neighborhoods like criminals
surreptitiously distributing flyers
that promote peace

but the necessity
of an urgent plea
calling both sides
to nonviolence
is a stark reminder

of just how much we stand
to lose
if either side
makes the first move.

The people have only words
to hurl
         or stones

but the police are armed
with tanks and guns.

When we run out of fliers
Papa and I are not far
from Lucas's apartment.
Before my shame can tie
my tongue and point my feet
toward retreat, I tell Papa
I need to see Lucas.

Papa agrees, but insists
on accompanying me to the door
and ensuring Lucas
will walk me home.
I bristle. This needless gallantry
could complicate
an already awkward visit.

When Lucas opens the door
        face brightening
my gaze drops
to the floor.

After Papa leaves
I step inside, searching
for the courage to say
what must be said.

As the door closes
behind me, tension crackles
in the air, snapping me
to attention.

Lucas's father, Herr Schumacher
        red-faced and
        thin-lipped
stands on the far side
of the room. His stare settles
briefly on Lucas

then he glances at me
nods curtly, stalks
from the room.

We had a surprise visit
from a Stasi officer, Lucas says
by way of explanation. *My father*
isn't exactly thrilled with me
at the moment.

It's happening
already.

It's fine, **Lucas says, his tone**
shifting—soft now
to comfort me.
He asked a few questions.
Had a look around.

Lucas gestures at the room

photos askew
on the walls

a handful of books splayed
on the floor

desk drawers and cupboards
ajar, revealing
disheveled contents.

Lucas, I'm so sorry.
They know—

        They're bluffing, he says.

They're not.

His head tilts slightly
as he looks at me
curiously.

I open my mouth to confess
but at that moment Herr Schumacher
strides into the room
scoops up the scattered
sections of a newspaper
before disappearing again
without a word.

Lucas closes the gap
between us, brushes my cheek
with the lightest touch.

Don't worry, he says, voice low.
*They've no proof
of anything. Tomorrow, we'll join
the demonstration. We'll march
as planned. Everything
will be fine.*

I desperately want to believe
he's right.

Late Monday afternoon
I'm alone in the apartment
trying to settle my nerves
as I prepare to go
meet Lucas. Papa won't be home
for dinner. He packed
an extra lunch this morning
so he could go directly to the church
after work, in case the police
won't let him back in the area
once he's left. And Mama
is still doing errands
after her shift.

This time, I scrawl a note
for Mama
let her know I've gone
     in case
     I don't come back
offer empty reassurances
of my safety, as if Lucas's presence
at my side will offer
any measure of protection
should the Stasi choose
to respond
with violence.

The police will never let us
get so far as downtown
if they know we have the banner
so we fold it lengthwise
and Lucas holds one end of it
while I hold the other. Then he turns
toward me, wrapping the banner
around his midriff. My hands

brush his chest, and I'm pierced
with sorrow
—if today's march doesn't convince
him to stay, there is no hope
for the future of us.

On the streetcar, other passengers
pay us no mind but I can't shake
the feeling they know
what we're up to—
as if they can see
through Lucas's bulky sweatshirt, know
it conceals contraband.

      Are any of them
      informers
      for the Stasi?

An unwelcome thought strikes
      like a sharp slap
      to the face:

            I am an informer
            for the Stasi.

The passengers ignore us.
As we near our stop, the truth
of what we're about to do

consumes me, and a reckless boldness
takes hold.

It should be nothing
to march, to ask—even
to demand
      change
but the presence of the military
and well-armed police
bear witness
that this regime
does not tolerate
demands.

Lucas spots a familiar face
in the sea of people.
We make our way
through the crowd
pleased to see Herr Weber

but instead of his usual gentle
smile, his expression is stern.
You shouldn't be here,
he says. *It's not safe.*

You're here, I say.

You're too young. They have
orders—he moves closer
places a hand on my shoulder
and one on Lucas's
pulling us into a huddle.
They have orders to
            shoot.
You must go home. Stay
safe.

Lucas chafes, perhaps thinking
he is not so young
or perhaps not believing
            or caring
about orders to shoot, but
I remember Brigitte's warning
remember the Stasi targeting
Herr Weber, remember
the magpie man threatening
Papa.

How do you know
about this order? Lucas asks.

—

A message, Herr Weber says.
Scrawled on a blackboard
at the university. I've no idea
who wrote it, but I believe it,
nonetheless.

Fear claws at me
        scratching
at my resolve
but Lucas assures Herr Weber
we'll steer clear of trouble
and leads me away.

My gaze
        darts about.

Military forces
and the Volkspolizei
weapons in hand

        here

                across the square

behind us.

A chant rises, citizens
calling out for restraint

        No violence!

The sound
runs the length
        of my spine
infusing me with fresh
determination, strengthening me
lifting

my head. I'm ready
to march.

Nikolaikirche: 9 October

The sacred text so often recited
by those who preach here
and those who worship
calls people to walk
in the way of peace.

It also calls them
to love mercy
and to seek justice

for mercy and justice
form the foundation
of peace.

The forces now encircling
my courtyard confirm
that the way of peace
is a difficult path

but as it has been said
peace
must be dared.

The church empties
into the square, pouring
people into spaces
too small to accommodate
them, nudging us into motion.

Lucas and I unwind the banner
　　my heart painted
　　in red letters
stretch it out between us
and allow ourselves to be carried
on the tide of demonstrators.

We've barely begun
when a disruption
to my right draws my attention:
　　a Stasi officer
wading through the crowd
directly toward me.

Before I can
　　think
move
　　　　run
he grabs the center
of our banner, snatches
it from our grasp, balls it up
as he stalks away, one end
　　　　trailing
along the cobblestones.

Lucas shouts at the officer's back
　*Reisefreiheit! Freedom
　to travel!*

The fierce edge in his voice
alarms me, revealing

how near he stands
        how near
        we *all* stand
to the verge
of violence.

I reach for his hand
squeeze it gently until anger melts
from his features, and we begin
to march again.

Reisefreiheit!

I echo the cry. Others nearby call
out as well, our voices uniting
in a bold banner
of sound.

The Volkspolizei
　　the People's Police
have forgotten
we *are* the people.

They stand ready to turn
their weapons on those
they're meant to serve

　　and yet
as the march progresses
their faces betray a measure
of uncertainty. Somehow
it makes them seem more
dangerous.

I scan the buildings lining
the street, search
for recessed doorways
　　alcoves
　　　　shadowy
　　　　corners
where Lucas and I might take cover
if they begin to shoot.

I'm not the only one
to sense the threat
　　and the opportunity
of their unease.

A new refrain builds
echoing
through the streets:

　　Wir sind das Volk!

We are the people.

We press on

step
      by step

fear
      falling away

shackles
             untethered

onward
until the security forces

      stand
      down.

We round the corner
at Tröndlinring
        again at Dittrichring
until the Runde Ecke
comes into view, looming
over us, dark windows
hurling reminders
of a repressive regime.

We shrink into ourselves
creep past as if at risk of waking
a sleeping bear.
Surely here
        at their headquarters
the Stasi will wield their weapons
        to break up the march.

But security forces
do not appear. Only a few police
remain
        scattered nearby.

We pass without incident

        spirits
            and footsteps
        surging forward.

On, we march, and on
        triumphant now
making our way the entire
length of the ring road.

Finally, radiant and buoyed
by the successful completion
of the loop, people break away
from the crowd to disperse

     resonant
into the night.

              I float
suspended
as by the lingering strains
of a symphonic
finale.

That was brilliant, Lucas says
as we turn toward home.
*What a way to wrap up
my years in the GDR.*

The notes of thrill
        cascade
crashing
to the pavement.

Lucas and I are bound
by our clasped hands. I let go
but he catches my fingers again
        grinning.
When our eyes meet
his smile fades.

What's wrong? he says.

Everything.
It's all so wrong

and if Lucas is caught
        or killed
at the border, it will be
my fault.

Surely you're not still planning—

The Stasi's little visit
was nothing. They just enjoy
shaking their filthy fists
in my face.

If only
that were true. If only
we could go back
to before
the magpie man.

The ache caused
by my duplicity
doubles
at the thought
of what I've thrown away.

I draw Lucas
from the jubilant crowd
find a quiet doorway
and sink onto cold stone

steps. Lucas sits beside me
and I force out the whole truth
despising
the self-justifying tone
dripping
from my words.

I explain what the Stasi
asked of me
      required
            of me
and what they would
      take from me
        and from Papa
if I failed
to yield to their demands.

I tried
to tell you. I did. But . . .

He nods. *The bikes?* he says.
The ladders? The shed?

I squeak out a reply. *I forgot*
about the bikes. They don't know
about the bikes.

He doesn't respond, so I grasp
at straws. *But like you said, they*
have no proof.

A chill creeps
from the steps, seeping
into my bones.

And my brother? Lucas says. *You told them
he's involved?*

When I don't deny it, he continues,
        voice growing as cold
as the stone.

*So you've put my brother
        and his wife
in danger.*

*We're all being watched
anyway, right?* My words are feeble
        pathetic
shaming me as they escape
from my lips.

Lucas is silent
for a long, painful moment
        his expression
        inscrutable.

By now, he says, *the Stasi
will have planted listening
devices in their apartment. Already
my brother and his wife may have incriminated
themselves unknowingly. Already
they may have offered the Stasi
more than enough evidence
        for their arrest.*

My eyes widen. *I never thought—*
My voice dies
as Lucas stares hard
into my eyes. His glare pierces
my soul, breaking me.

He rises and strides
away.

      I lose him
in the crowd.

I walk
>   slowly
my steps
heavy.

When I finally drag myself
into the apartment
Mama and Papa bombard me
with
>   questions
>   exclamations
>   admonishments
for which I can drum up
no response. I remain silent
until the barrage ends.

Then I confess

the magpie
>   and his threats
Lucas's plan
and my own
>   betrayal.

I choke out the last
>   worst
truth before my throat closes.

Mama wraps me
in her arms, forgetting
>   at least for now
my sin of sneaking away
to the march. Papa stomps
around the room, railing
>   not at me
but at the Party, the Stasi,
Herr Honecker, and the damned

brokenness of it all.

When he's done
he crouches at my side
lifts my chin
with his hand.

This, he says, voice
so fierce it breaks. *This*
is why we must never
give
up.

At school, Frau Stein reprimands me
for my failures

failure to rise
failure to focus
failure to behave
      as a responsible
      socialist
      citizen.

No doubt, if she knew
what I'd done to Lucas
she would commend me.

The day seems endless
the glacial passing of time
made worse by constant thoughts
of what might've been, if only
I were stronger.
            Braver.

When classes end for the day
I set off for Herr Weber's
and a new torment
takes over.

      How am I to face Lucas?

Those moments
            between

      once savored
now stark
            bitter
reminders of all I've thrown away.

The tram reaches my stop

but I remain seated.
I'll have to apologize
to Herr Weber for skipping
my lesson, but for now I ride
    aimless.

Shari Green

I stumble through the days
at school as if wandering
in thick fog, any value
of the lessons obscured.

What Lucas and I had

      and could've had
      in the future

was both cast aside
by me
and stolen
by the Stasi.

I should despise myself and curse
my country, but hate
takes more energy
than I can muster.

Instead, I turn to my piano
whenever I'm at home
surround myself
in the heavy comfort
of Beethoven's most moody
compositions. I find refuge
in his *Adagio Cantabile*
and hide there for hours.

On Friday, when Papa arrives home
he brings news:

the State has released many
who were imprisoned.

Change is coming, he says.
I can feel it.

Something has already changed
in Mama. Since my confession
her eyes blaze with a fierceness
reminiscent of the woman
she was in the photos
from college days. Perhaps
that moment was Mama's
        enough.

Papa decides we must go out
as if our small apartment
        drenched in the melancholy
        of Beethoven
cannot possibly contain
the optimism bubbling
inside him.

We go for a stroll downtown
        the air cool, the day bright
despite a gray sky.
Around me, energy flits
like fireflies, glinting
on the faces of passersby.
Snippets of conversation dart
into my ears—words
        that ought to be
        whispered
now spoken freely on the street.

Honecker should resign.

> *Elections have never*
> *been fair.*

The Western
news channel . . .

I want to claim the freedom
strangers dare to flaunt
as if they've no fear
of reprisals

and yet
I am anything
but free.

Mama, of course, knows.

Go, she says. *Talk to Lucas.*
He grew up here—he knows
what it's like. Maybe
he'll understand.

I knock

wait

knock again.

Surely he didn't go
to Berlin—not knowing
the Stasi are aware
of his plans

but I fear
he's susceptible to
the intoxicating thrill
of danger. Is his brother
the same?

Even now
Lucas may be wrestling
with ladders.

Even now
border guards may be hoisting
their rifles, aiming
at his back.

My heart
shatters.

I push away my plate, dinner
uneaten. I must try again.

Mama and Papa say nothing
until my hand
touches the doorknob.

Mäuschen, Papa says,
one word
holding a world.

I look back.

If he's gone, Papa says,
it was his choice.

If Lucas is gone, I can't help
but think it a *foolish* choice.

It's also a choice
that will crush me
whether or not
he is successful.

Frau Schumacher cracks open the door
wary, perhaps, of another visit from the Stasi.

When she sees me, she lets out a breath
tells me only that Lucas
                                            is not home.

Before I can respond, the door clicks shut.

Nikolaikirche: 16 October

Empowered,
the people gather
in streets surrounding my courtyard,
crowds doubled since last week
demonstrations mounting
in momentous crescendo.

It's only a matter of time before the people realize
the impossible
has become possible

walls
can be torn down.

The Stasi, it seems, were prepared
for everything except
candles, prayer, and song.

Despite the worry and shame gnawing
on my gut, I'm determined
to march again for a country

that no longer
      drives its citizens to reckless
      schemes of escape

nor forces them to choose
      between integrity and duty

      or between family
         and friend.

Both Papa and I long
for a moment of calm
so we set out early
      Mama with us
in hopes of claiming seats
in the sanctuary.

Half a block from home
I hear a voice call my name
      low and melodious
      like the song
      of a blackbird.
Across the street, a familiar
long-legged figure
      hands in pockets, wavy hair falling
over his face. I break
from Mama and Papa
and hurry
to meet Lucas.

The air between us is thick
with a new awkwardness
putting a stopper in the flood
of my apologies.

In the end there are few words
exchanged, but there is a promise:

I'm staying, Lucas says,
    at least
    for now.

When Lucas leans in
    places the gentlest
    of kisses
    on my forehead
it feels like farewell

until his fingers
brush my cheek
and his lips
find mine.

Crowds prevent the tram
from continuing
so Mama, Papa, Lucas, and I
    disembark
inch our way toward the square
already overflowing
with demonstrators.

There's no chance
we'll get into the church
but Papa says marching
is as much a prayer
as bowing our heads
and opening our hearts.

When the doors
of the Nikolaikirche open
music spills out and floats
over us, following
as we march
unhindered
    a river surging
through the streets.

I reach for Lucas
    and he takes my hand.
On my other side, Mama links
one arm with mine, the other
with Papa's. Her face shines.

The future of Germany
is being decided
    right now
    right here
in Leipzig, and we
are making it happen.

The truth of it expands
within me
      like the moment
of delicious anticipation
before a symphony.
The conductor raises
a baton, and the orchestra
stills
      instruments
      poised.

The inevitability
of change
infuses the air.

     I breathe
it in, fill my lungs
with empowering

     life-giving

hope.

AUTHOR'S NOTE

In *Song of Freedom, Song of Dreams*, the voice of Saint Nicholas Church makes reference to three quotes. The first is from Karl Barth: "To clasp the hands in prayer is the beginning of an uprising against the disorder of the world."[1] The second is from Dietrich Bonhoeffer: "There is no way to peace along the way of safety. For peace must be dared. It is the great venture. It can never be safe."[2] And the third, attributed to a senior Stasi official: when asked why they had not quashed the Monday protests as they had all others, he reportedly said, "We had no contingency plan for song." No contingency plan for song! It was this phrase that sparked my fascination with the idea of music as an act of resistance and led me to dive into the history of Leipzig's peaceful protests. While I was unable to verify the exact quote, it may be simply a variation of this one attributed to Erich Mielke: "We were prepared for everything but not for prayers and candles."[3] Regardless, it became the impetus for Helena's story.

The main characters in this story are fictional, but the historical backdrop and political events are real. In the former German Democratic Republic (East Germany), elections weren't fair, people weren't free to leave the country at will, and the Stasi—the secret police—kept close watch on citizens, employing a huge network of unofficial informants. Under the ruling Socialist Unity Party (the SED), there was no room for dissident speech or actions. There was no room for dreamers or dreams.

Helena says her dreams—her desire to experience life beyond the GDR—began with a gunshot, when she overheard at age 10 the story of a boy

---

[1] Karl Barth, *The Christian Life: Church Dogmatics IV.4*, as quoted in *Vital Christianity: Spirituality, Justice, and Christian Practice*, eds. David L. Weaver-Zercher and William H. Willimon (Edinburgh, UK: T&T Clark, 2005), 141.

[2] John de Gruchy, ed., *Dietrich Bonhoeffer: Witness to Jesus Christ* (Minneapolis, MN: Fortress Press, 1991), 132.

[3] Doris Mundus, *Leipzig 1989: A Chronicle* (Susanne Mundus, trans. Leipzig: Lehmstedt Verlag, 2009), 25.

who was killed by border guards. In this case, I shifted the historical timeline to suit the story: Helena would've been 10 in 1983, but in fact, Jörg Hartmann, 10, and Lothar Schleusener, 13, were fatally shot by border guards in Berlin in March of 1966.

Many citizens of the GDR desperately wanted out. However, many others wanted to stay but longed for reforms. The Monday peace prayers and demonstrations brought both groups together, united by their common desire for a better life, a better country. The peace prayers, which had been happening at Saint Nicholas Church in Leipzig since 1982, gave people the freedom and opportunity to discuss subjects they dared not mention elsewhere, and their discontent found focus and inspiration.

On September 4, 1989, the day of the fall trade fair in Leipzig, Western media had been given permission to film in the city, and the peace prayers ended up on West German television, spreading the word about what was happening in Leipzig. Demonstrations grew, both in Leipzig and in other East German cities. On October 7, the fortieth anniversary of the founding of the GDR, celebrations throughout the country were marked by violence. The tipping point came in Leipzig on October 9, when the government determined to crack down on the protests using whatever means necessary. Despite fears of a brutal response like in Tiananmen Square in Beijing earlier that year, the citizens went ahead with the demonstration, with church and group leaders urging all to refrain from violence. That the police and security forces stood down is something of a miracle, but the sheer number of demonstrators and their absolute commitment to nonviolence won out. That evening, the people marched the complete distance of Leipzig's ring road without incident.

On October 18, the leader of the SED, Erick Honecker, resigned after being overthrown by Egon Krenz at a meeting of the Politburo. The demonstrations in Leipzig grew to half a million people, and their demands became bolder as they called for more radical change: *the Wall must go!* They also continued to call for nonviolence.

Finally, on November 7, Erich Mielke, the Minister of State Security (head of the Stasi), recognized the government could no longer resist the pressure from the people. By the next day, he and the entire Politburo had resigned. On November 9, revised travel regulations were quickly drafted, and the document was read aloud by Günter Schabowski at a press conference. When asked about when the changes were to take effect, he appeared uncertain but replied "immediately."[4] East Germans flooded to the Berlin Wall, catching border guards by surprise. Most guards decided to let citizens cross. The next day, all East German borders opened, and people could travel freely to the West. The Wall had fallen.

Free elections took place in the GDR in March 1990, and on October 3, 1990, Germany reunified. The former GDR territory became five new states in the Federal Republic of Germany.

Who could've imagined that weekly prayer meetings would grow into massive protests? Who could've foreseen that the Wall, once seemingly so insurmountable, would be brought down by the power of candles, prayers, and song? Citizens united for change, determined to remain peaceful, and undaunted by the threat of violence from a corrupt government, ultimately brought down the state, reshaping the future of Germany.

---

[4] Schabowski, Günter. "Press Conference in the GDR International Press Center 6:53–7:01 p.m.," Recorded November 9, 1989. The Wilson Center Digital Archive, last modified November 20, 2011, accessed April 5, 2023, http://digitalarchive.wilsoncenter.org/document/113049

ACKNOWLEDGMENTS

I wrote this book in the midst of the most difficult time of my life, while my daughter underwent treatment for cancer, and then later, after she passed away. It was a time that demanded more courage than our family had ever before required, a time that found us clinging desperately to hope. When there was little hope, we needed courage all the more.

Looking back now, I find it interesting that Helena's story is also one of courage and hope—coincidence? Maybe, maybe not. This I know: sitting beside a hospital bed while my daughter slept during chemo was far from *normal*, but having a notebook and pen in my hand while I sat there offered me a tiny glimpse of normalcy. And so I wandered back and forth between my upside-down world and 1989 Leipzig, and I wrote, and hoped, and scrabbled about for scraps of courage. It truly feels like a dream to know the story that emerged during that time will soon be a real book (and now, as you read this, it is!). Here's to dreams. Here's to courage. Here's to hope.

Thank you to my wonderful editor, Patty Rice, and to the excellent team at Andrews McMeel, especially Danys Mares, Dave Shaw, Shona Burns, and Tiffany Meairs (thank you for the exquisite cover, Tiffany). Working with all of you is a joy.

To my extraordinary agent, Amy Bishop—thank you for your guidance, wisdom, and compassion; I'm so fortunate to have you in my corner.

To Heather Wik—thank you for helping me hear a song of hope throughout the most difficult year of my life; I love you, sis. To Kristin Reynolds, my comrade in sorrow and in hope—thank you for all the virtual hugs and late-night messaging as we walked that awful road together; peace to you, my friend. To Kip Wilson, dear friend and CP extraordinaire (now with bonus! German language assistance)—thank you for your excellent feedback and for your love and support. To Janet Smith—I love you; thank you for believing in me (I can't wait till we meet Tennant). To my PitchWars14 family—thank you for your generous and unending support. And to the many friends, colleagues, and strangers who shared light and love when I most needed it, thank you; your kindness meant the world to me.

I'm grateful to all who helped me track down information or provided assistance and feedback on specific aspects of this story, especially Ernst Leitz, Graham Maclagan (Info Tech, Vancouver Island Regional Library), Dianne Mason, Annett Stuetz, Lutz Weiner (Collections/Documentation, *Schulmuseum*, Leipzig), and Kip Wilson. Their help was brilliant; any errors are my own.

Love to all my family, especially "my boys"—Nick, Tom, Jesse, and Chris—four of the finest people I know. And always, Skip . . . look at us, still standing despite the storm; I'm so glad you're by my side as we walk through the beautiful and terrible happenings of this life. Lovelovelove.

Finally, to all whose lives have been impacted by cancer or, like Helena, by oppression and injustice, I send you light and love. May your heart be tuned to brave music, and may you always hear the persistent song of hope.

GLOSSARY

Befiehl du deine Wege: a hymn, translated as *Entrust your way*

Ein feste Burg: a hymn, translated as *A mighty fortress*

FDJ (Freie Deutsche Jugend): Free German Youth

Frau: woman, missus (Mrs. or Ms.)

Fräulein: young woman (Miss)

Friedensgebete: peace prayers

Freiheit: freedom

Freie Wahlen: free elections

Gewandhaus: the concert hall in Leipzig

Herr: man, mister (Mr.)

Hochschule für Musik: college of music

Liebchen: sweetheart

Mäuschen: little mouse; a term of endearment

Nein: no

Ratskeller: a bar, restaurant, or nightclub located in the basement of a town hall

Redefreiheit: freedom of speech

Reisefreiheit: freedom to travel

Runde Ecke: literally, round corner; headquarters of the Stasi in Leipzig

Stasi (Ministerium für Staatssicherheit): the East German Ministry for State Security

Volkspolizei: the People's Police

Volkszeitung: the People's Newspaper; Leipzig's local newspaper

Wie schön leuchtet: a hymn, translated as *How lovely shines*

Wir sind das Volk: we are the people

SELECTED SOURCES

Bartee, Wayne C. *A Time to Speak Out: The Leipzig Citizen Protests and the Fall of East Germany.* Westport, CT: Praeger, 2000.

Bösch, Frank, ed. *A History Shared and Divided: East and West Germany Since the 1970s.* English-language edition. Translated by Jennifer Walcoff Neuheiser. Oxford, NY: Berghahn Books, 2018.

Chronik der Mauer. Chronicle text by Dr. Hans-Hermann Hertle and Dr. Burghard Ciesla. Translation by Tim Jones. https://www.chronik -der-mauer.de/

Funder, Anna. *Stasiland: Stories from Behind the Berlin Wall.* New York, NY: HarperCollins, 2011.

Geck, Martin. *Johann Sebastian Bach: Life and Work.* English-language edition. Translated by John Hargraves. Orlando, FL: Harcourt, 2006.

Schabowski, Günter. "Press Conference in the GDR International Press Center 6:53–7:01 p.m.," Recorded November 9, 1989. The Wilson Center Digital Archive, last modified November 20, 2011, accessed April 5, 2023, http://digitalarchive.wilsoncenter.org/document/113049

Hensel, Jana. *After the Wall: Confessions from an East German Childhood and the Life that Came Next.* Translated by Jefferson Chase. New York, NY: PublicAffairs, 2008.

Müller-Enbergs, Helmut. *Die inoffiziellen Mitarbeiter (MfS-Hand-buch).* Berlin: Hg. BstU, 2008. http://www.nbn-resolving.org/ urn:nbn:de:0292-97839421302647

Mundus, Doris. *Leipzig 1989: A Chronicle.* Translated by Susanne Mundus. Leipzig: Lehmstedt Verlag, 2009.

Religion & Ethics Newsweekly. November 6, 2009. "The Rev. Christian Fuhrer Extended Interview." https://www.pbs.org/wnet/religionandethics/2009/11/06/november-6-2009-the-rev-christian-fuhrer-extended-interview/4843/

Rückel, Robert, ed. *GDR-Guide: A Journey to a Bygone State*. 2nd ed. Berlin: DDR Museum Verlag GmbH, 2012.

Sarott, Mary Elise. *The Collapse: The Accidental Opening of the Berlin Wall*. Reprint edition. New York, NY: Basic Books, 2015.

Smith, Patricia. *Revolution Revisited: Behind the Scenes in East Germany, 1989*. Dog Ear Publishing, 2014.

Starcevic, Nesha. 1989. "Communist Politburo Resigns; Reformers Elevated; Krenz Reaffirmed." Associated Press, November. https://apnews.com/article/64dde36b3e58211b31d55cfbd6cc5940

Vaizey, Hester. *Born in the GDR: Living in the Shadow of the Wall*. Oxford, UK: Oxford University Press, 2014.

Wolfgang Kenntemich, dir. *Das war die DDR – Eine Geschichte des anderen Deutschland*. Berlin: Manfred Durniok Produktion, 1992. Film.

Gerd Kroske and Andreas Voigt, dirs. *Leipzig im Herbst*. Amherst, MA: DEFA Film Library, 1989. Film.

Shari Green is the author of several novels in verse, including the ALA Schneider Family Book Award winner, *Macy McMillan and the Rainbow Goddess*. Her books have been included on international "best of" lists and nominated for multiple state and provincial readers' choice programs. Shari is also a poet, musician, and former nurse. She can often be found wandering the beaches or forest trails near her home on Vancouver Island, BC, Canada.

Photo by: Pedersen Arts Photography